THE
BOY
IN THE
SMOKE

Also by Rachel Faturoti

Sadé and Her Shadow Beasts

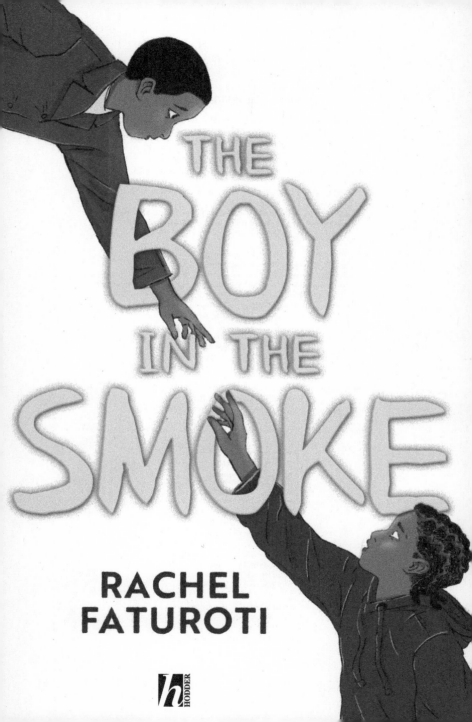

THE BOY IN THE SMOKE

RACHEL FATUROTI

HODDER CHILDREN'S BOOKS

First published in Great Britain in 2023 by Hodder & Stoughton Limited

1 3 5 7 9 10 8 6 4 2

A CIP catalogue record for this book
is available from the British Library.

ISBN 978 1 444 96358 8

Typeset in Baskerville by Palimpsest Book Production Limited, Falkirk, Stirlingshire
Printed and bound in Great Britain by
Clays Ltd, Elcograf S.p.A.

The paper and board used in this book are made from wood from responsible sources.

MIX
Paper from
responsible sources
FSC® C104740
FSC
www.fsc.org

Hodder Children's Books
An imprint of
Hachette Children's Group
Part of Hodder & Stoughton Limited
Carmelite House
50 Victoria Embankment
London EC4Y 0DZ

An Hachette UK Company
www.hachette.co.uk

www.hachettechildrens.co.uk

*This book is dedicated to the people I meet
each week at the Food Hub.*

Chapter One

Monday

'Isaiah!' Dad calls from somewhere in the flat. 'Isaiah! Time to get up for school. I've got a surprise for you!'

A notification pops up on my phone with a video. *Memory from three years ago.* Firming our frosty flat, my hand slips out from under the covers to play the video.

'Happy birthday to you! Happy birthday to you! Happy birthday to Isaiah! Happy birthday to you!' the crowd of my friends and family shout as the glow from my ten birthday candles light up my face.

'Go on, make a wish, Isaiah,' Mum says.

'I don't believe in wishes.' Impatiently, I blow out the candles. 'And I've already got everything I want.'

Dad reveals another present from behind his back. 'Not everything. I hope you like it, son.'

I tear off the shiny blue wrapping paper. 'Yes! You got me Lio the Robot.'

'I knew he'd love it,' Mum whispers to Dad.

I shiver, tugging on my worn-out grey dressing gown over my jumper. I sink deeper under my thin bedcovers.

'Have you switched on the boiler yet?' He doesn't reply. 'Dad?'

When I don't get an answer, I slide out of my single bed, feeling the cold through the layers of clothes.

Our flat doesn't have many pictures on the walls, even though we moved in a year ago. We're still 'settling in', but, if I'm being honest, we don't have much to settle with. It takes me seconds to walk from my bedroom to the closed white living-room door. Our flat is tiny.

'Dad, are you in there?' I ask, peeking through the keyhole as he moves past in his black coat with the odd button.

Dad thinks he's surprising me, but I saw the Savers bag with the birthday balloons hidden behind the small TV I tried to fix yesterday.

'Just one second, son.' Dad's voice travels through the thin walls.

'How's your back?' I question, jiggling the cold metal handle.

'It's . . . great.'

'Really?'

Dad chuckles. 'You got me. It's *better* today.'

The door flies open.

'But today isn't about me. It's about you.' Dad's body stiffens slightly in the doorway. He tugs at his overgrown beard. 'Happy thirteenth birthday, son! Make a wish.' A small cupcake with icing rests in his hand. I didn't believe in wishes before, but I do now.

'Thanks, Dad.' I tug my dressing gown tighter around my body, marching forward. 'I know what I'm gonna wish for.'

I wish that Dad and I get more money so we can afford things and that Mum moves back from Berlin after she finishes her architecture programme.

'I've got another surprise for you,' Dad says, limping away from the door.

Except for the red birthday banner and the balloon, our living room is exactly the same, with Dad's lumpy second-hand pull-out sofa bed, the small, rocky wooden side table Dad made and the tiny box TV.

I pick up the large, wrapped present with a birthday card stuck to the front. I open the card first.

How many Isaiahs does it take to screw in a lightbulb? None, because Isaiah invented it. Happy birthday, son.

I tear the wrapping paper. There are three second-hand books: one on inventions, one 'how to fix it' guide and another on how things like 3D printers work.

The last present is a mini whiteboard. I'd wished for a tablet, but I don't say that obviously.

'And that's not all,' he adds. 'After we get your hair done at your uncle's, I'm taking you to eat at Fucchinis.'

'What? Is that it? No dinosaur?' I say, keeping a straight face.

Dad ruffles my hair, laughing. 'Always the jokester.'

'Fucchinis is cool.' I hug him. 'Thanks, Dad, but how did you get the mon—'

'It's your birthday,' he replies, smiling, but I know he's managing the pain. 'I did what I needed to do. And this also came for you.'

It must be from Mum.

Dad's short black locs flop around as he picks up the card left on his sofa bed.

I prise the card out of his hand, looking around him for the drone. 'Did it come with anything else?'

Dad shakes his head. 'No, just this.'

'Oh,' I say.

'Why?' Dad frowns. 'Did your mother promise you something?'

'It's all right, Dad.'

Mum promised she'd get me a drone for my big thirteenth birthday and not just any drone, but the DR4X.

The king of drones. Mum *always* keeps her promises when it comes to getting my birthday presents – plus I told her about the drone months ago.

I take the card out of the envelope.

To Isaiah, my smart son,

Happy 13th birthday! I'm so sorry I can't be there with you, but I'm there in spirit and hopefully I'll be able to come to Shepten once I've settled.

Love, your mum.

'Go and get ready for school,' Dad says, sitting down carefully on the sofa as the sweat builds around his hairline. 'I don't need you to be late – again.'

'We've got a late special assembly today,' I half lie. 'Let's do those stretching exercises you learnt at physio first.'

'Are you sure about that?' Dads asks, shooting me a glance. 'Because I didn't get a message from school about the assembly being late.'

Dad tugs at the end of my messy cornrows.

'All right, it's *not* late,' I admit.

'We always have to tell each other the truth,' he replies. 'It's just us two.'

It went from *three*: Mum, Dad and me to us two. When they separated two years ago, Mum got her own place, and I saw her all the time, but now she's in Berlin studying and I don't see her.

'We can just do *one* exercise then,' I offer.

I unfurl the yoga mat on the floor and Dad lies back on it with his legs stretched out in front of him. 'Just one exercise, Isaiah.'

'Are you ready?' I ask, and he nods as I take one of his legs, bending it towards his body as the other leg stays flat against the mat. I can feel how stiff Dad's muscles are. 'How does that feel? Tight?'

'Yes,' he murmurs between breaths. 'You shouldn't be . . . doing this for me.'

'Breathe.' I grip behind the knee. 'Go.' Dad pushes against my hands for five seconds. He strains, gasping through his teeth before pausing. 'Well done, Dad.' I slowly move his knee closer to his chest and hold for a few seconds before doing the same stretch to the other leg. 'Done.'

'Thanks, son.' He sits on the sofa, resting his feet on the floor.

'Don't you have a job interview today?' I say, rolling the mat up.

'Yes, I do. It's an admin role for a construction company, working from home. I can manage a few hours here and there.'

'You're going to smash it.'

'It's not the best, but it'll do for now.' He nudges me with his slipper. 'Time for you to go and get ready.'

Leaving Dad, I go straight to the boiler and rotate the switch, but nothing happens. With my hand shoved right in the back, I open the boiler valves and hear the water filling up. The spinning black arrow for the pressure twitches until it reaches a certain number. I close the valves and switch the boiler on.

I brush my teeth and shower at the same time; we don't waste water. The mould at the corner of the shower grows every day like liquid seeping into paper. I scrub it away, but it comes back every time. Our landlord blames it on our flat being Victorian, but it's because there's no bathroom fan and the window doesn't open. He won't pay to fix anything.

Spitting out the toothpaste, the water mixes with it, dyeing it blue as it swirls down the drain like a mini tornado. 'I'm done!'

In a minute, I've got on my white shirt, black trousers, blazer, and striped tie that I shorten.

Me: Hi mum. are u awake?
is the drone almost here???

'Isaiah!' Kieran shouts from outside the flat.

I walk out of the door and lean over the landing. I can only see the top of Kieran's curly high top as he bends down to tie the laces on his school shoes.

'Kieran!'

'Happy birthday!' he shouts as he lifts his head up. 'You need to hurry up if you wanna go on my scooter before school.'

Kieran rests on his new Pure Wind second-generation electric scooter with the blue ambient lights at the bottom, regenerative braking technology, USB charging port *and* up to 8.5 hours charge time.

I close the front door and rummage through the empty kitchen cupboards, find the last pack of oats for Dad and mix them with water from the tap. I count down two minutes on the microwave.

The hot bowl burns my hand as I take it out without a cloth. *I'm running out of scooter time.* I put the bowl with a spoon inside on the side table. 'Good luck with the interview.'

'Thanks,' he replies, lifting his head up. 'Have a great day at school! We'll continue your birthday celebrations afterwards.'

Chapter Two

We burst through the green school gates with our ties flapping behind us.

'Mr Oni and Mr Alders,' Mr Sankofa enunciates, his slight Ghanaian accent flavouring our names. 'You're late. Do you know what that means?'

'I'm the reason we're late. Sorry, Mr Sankofa,' I apologise, trying to butter him up. 'You can't really give us detentions on my birthday, can you?'

Mr Sankofa steps forward with his finger pointed, but the anger leaves him, so I know we're off the hook. 'This will be your *last* warning, Isaiah. I take my job as a teacher very seriously.'

Ting-a-ling.

'Laters, sir!' I shout, running off to our IT lesson.

As we're about to walk in, someone clears their throat behind us. 'You can go in, Kieran,' Mrs Morris says, 'but I need to talk to Isaiah for a second.'

Putting on a cheesy smile, I spin round and face Mrs Morris, the welfare officer. Her thick eyebrows rise and she blows a black curl out of her eye, frustrated.

'Firstly, hoodie off.'

With my hand hovering over the zip, I try one more time. 'Miss, are those new earrings?'

'I'm not falling for none of that sweet talk, nuh uh.' She shakes her head. 'This is the *second* time you've been late in the last week with the *wrong* uniform. Where's your jumper?'

The only jumper I have is still wet at home, drying slowly on the radiator, but I don't tell Mrs Morris this.

'And what's that on your school shoes?' she asks, pointing down, and I also look down, pretending like I didn't draw graffiti on them to cover the tears.

I flash another grin. 'But, Mrs Morris, didn't you say before in assembly that creativity is important?'

A small smile plays on Mrs Morris's lips and I know I've escaped more questions. 'You're too bright. Go on, get in your lesson. I expect that paint to be washed off by tomorrow.'

'Of course I'll do that, miss.'

Inside the room, Mr Iyer, our IT teacher, stands in front of the class, taking the register.

'Kesia. Kesia?'

'Sir, I think she's got an appointment,' Mary answers, fixing her headband.

Everyone knows that Kesia has sickle cell so the appointment might be for that or something else. I wouldn't know though because Kesia and I don't talk a lot.

'Right, right,' Mr Iyer replies. *Sniff.* 'Kirsty?'

Kieran, Fredrick and I are tucked in the back of the computer room, where Mr Iyer can't see.

They give me 'birthday beats', raining thirteen soft punches on my arms.

'Get off me, man.' I laugh, sitting down in between them.

Kirsty spins round in her chair, playing with her auburn braid. 'Happy birthday, Isaiah.'

Fredrick's eyes go as wide as a cartoon character's. He swears she's the prettiest girl in our class – even the *whole* school. I crack a smile. 'Thanks, Kirsty.'

'Did your drone come?' Kieran asks, while Fredrick stares at the back of Kirsty's head.

I check my phone for a message from Mum, but there's nothing. *Why isn't she texting me back?*

Mr Iyer sniffs, uncapping his whiteboard pen. 'Attention to the front, please.' The word HTML is on the board. 'You should each have already decided what business you want to base your website on. You will be creating websites for your businesses using HTML.'

'Not yet,' I reply, putting my phone away. 'But she did say it would be here today. Did I tell you guys that it has up to thirty minutes of flight time, can be controlled with a phone, has an HD camera—'

Mr Iyer clears his throat, interrupting. 'Are you boys listening back there? What was I saying?'

'Yeah, sir,' I answer. 'HTML stands for Hypertext Markup Language and I know about adding links to a webpage, structuring a webpage and all that.'

People from my class whisper at the relaxed smile on Mr Iyer's face.

'Excellent, Isaiah,' he praises. 'That's what I like to hear, students who take initiative to learn outside the classroom. I can't wait to see your fantastic website, Isaiah, and to hear what your business will be.'

Fredrick makes a noise out of his large nostrils. 'Show off.'

'Looks like someone's got a case of the itis,' Kieran jokes. 'Jealous-itis.'

'Crybaby-itis,' I add.

Fredrick chuckles. 'Whatever.'

'We will be looking at the audience and purposes of websites today,' Mr Iyer continues.

'What's your business?' Kieran asks. 'Mine is going to be customising trainers. You gave me the idea.'

Kieran doesn't know why I had to draw on my trainers. I can't tell him that Dad couldn't afford new ones. 'I've got loads of ideas, but I'm still deciding.'

I don't have *any* ideas.

'We'll start with the purpose of a website,' Mr Iyer says. 'Not only does the information on your site need to be relevant, but it needs to be accurate too.' *Sniff.* 'Who is your target audience? Can you tell me the target audiences for these two sites?'

One is a news site and the other one is for children.

'Yes, Kirsty.'

'Ermm, one is boring and doesn't have a lot of colours,' she answers. 'It's something my mum would go on. It also has more information on it compared to the other one. Is it for adults?'

'Yes.' *Sniff.* Mr Iyer ignores the rest of the hands, answering the next one himself. 'The other one is targeted at children. I have saved a file in the website folder. By yourselves, I want you to write down who you think the target audience is for each site listed and why. Does anyone have any questions?'

A few people raise their hands, but Mr Iyer has turned back to the board. 'Get started, everybody. Your homework for next lesson is to think of different features that would help create a successful website and you *must* explain why each feature is important,' Mr Iyer says.

I need to think of a website idea by next lesson or I'm in trouble.

Chapter Three

The high street is busy late afternoon and getting to Uncle Kwame's barbershop is like playing a real-life game of Tetris.

'How'd the interview go?' I quiz Dad as we walk there.

'Good, I think,' Dad replies, hands tucked under his armpits. 'The manager, Rick, seemed impressed by my previous experience. If I'm starting work soon, I'll need your uncle Kwame to get rid of this scruff.' He touches his rough beard.

I can't count on my fingers how many interviews Dad's been on, but I know he'll get one. *It took the Wright brothers many tries before they invented the first successful flying machine.*

Dad whistles as we continue down the road and speaks to himself. 'I'll need to dig out some smart clothes too. First impressions are important.'

Ahead is the green barbershop with the long windows at the front and 'Kwame's' in fancy letters. Customers jam the barbershop to the brim and the queue spills out on to the street.

'My brother,' Uncle Kwame says to my dad before speaking to me. 'Young blood, happy thirteenth birthday.'

'Thanks, Unc. Am I getting thirteen presents then?' I ask, flashing a smile. The other men in the barbershop laugh. 'See. Everyone agrees.'

Amused, Uncle Kwame shakes his head and offers me his hand to slap, and he hugs my dad as if this is their first time seeing each other in ages, but they're just very close. Uncle Kwame isn't my blood uncle. Dad and Unc met at university and have been like brothers ever since. Dad is an only child – same as me.

Joseph, one of the barbers, taps a recently vacated black chair. 'Take a seat. No queuing for the birthday boy.' He blow-dries out my big afro and greases my scalp to prepare it for the cornrows as Dad takes the chair next to me.

To Mum: hello ???

'What have you got planned for the rest of your big day?' Joseph asks, parting my hair in a zigzag pattern.

'Dad's taking me out to Fucchinis. You know it?'

'They've got some *nice* garlic bread there.' He hums, probably picturing it.

'Yeah. No one can touch Fucchinis' garlic bread – it's the best.'

Uncle Kwame shakes out a black bib, securing it around Dad's neck. He switches the razor on and brushes Dad's beard with a small black brush. The razor buzzes in the background as I check the features of my new drone again on my phone.

We're done before I know it. I touch the neat edges of my fresh zigzag cornrows, which resemble sparks of electricity on my head. 'These look nice. Thanks, man.'

'Happy birthday, Isaiah,' Uncle Kwame says, producing a long black box from behind his back.

Snatching it out of his hands, I dig through the box and take out the black retro Jordans that I've wanted for *years*. 'How did you know?'

'You've spoken about them plenty, so I searched on StockQ and bid for them. I won't tell you how much it cost in the end, but the important thing is that you got them, young blood.'

'Wow! Thanks, Unc.' I turn the trainers around, admiring them. 'These are too clean. Watch when Kieran and Fredrick see them.'

Uncle Kwame grins. 'They can replace the ones you got on.'

Dad's eyes shoot down, staring at my torn trainers like

he's only just noticed them. 'Thanks, Kwame. We'll see you later. Don't want to miss our reservation.'

As we're walking away, Dad discreetly checks his wallet. Frown lines form around his mouth and then he checks his phone.

'Dad, are you all right?'

'Yes, just a little tired.' Sweat gathers along Dad's brow. 'I maybe need to take a quick nap.'

Other people don't see the signs he's in pain, but I do. Dad has been faking it for me and a 'quick nap' usually means his body is exhausted. It's shutting down and there's nothing he can do about it.

'We don't need to go to Fucchinis today.'

'You're going! I won't ruin your big day. I asked Kieran's mum in case I couldn't take you. I just . . . can't take you. Kieran and Fredrick will be there too – sounds fun, doesn't it?'

My stomach knots like a rope. This will be the first birthday I'm celebrating without my mum *or* dad. 'Yeah, sounds fun.'

When Dad drops me off at Fucchinis, Kieran, Kieran's mum and Fredrick are already at the table.

'*Joyeux anniversaire!*' they all shout, which makes me feel a bit better.

Kieran is half Congolese and half Dutch, so I'm used to hearing different languages.

'Lemme see your trainers,' Fredrick says as I lift up my tracksuit leg to show him the fresh Jordans. 'I wanted them ones. They're sick.'

Kieran takes a picture of my whole fit from my fresh cornrows down to the new Jordans.

A man in a white shirt and black bowtie comes to take our order. I scan the menu, noticing the prices. 'I'll have a Coke and the pepperoni pizza, please.'

'Don't you wanna get the garlic bread?' Kieran asks, giving me a funny look. 'You're *always* chatting about it.'

'I'm all right with pizza.'

Kieran's mum shakes her head slightly, turning to the waiter. 'We'll have some extra-cheesy garlic bread for the birthday boy too.'

'Wonderful,' he replies, and takes all the menus from the table. 'I'll be back shortly with your drinks.'

I smile at Kieran's mum.

'Have you got anything else planned for your birthday, Isaiah?' she asks.

Years ago, we always made my birthday special.

'Not yet,' I reply. 'But I'm waiting for my mum to send me this drone. It's the best. And she might be coming to Shepten to see me soon.'

'It would be lovely to meet her when she's over from Berlin.'

'Wheels is doing parkour in Berlin next!' Kieran exclaims.

Wheels, or Shawn Harley, is our favourite Australian extreme sporter.

'Crikey, throw some shrimp on the barbie,' Kieran jokes.

'Blimey, mate!' I join in until we're just saying random things at each other.

'Here we are,' the waiter says, putting down our drinks and extra-cheesy garlic bread. As I take a bite, Fredrick asks, 'Have you heard of the worm challenge? The guy eats fifty worms, but some come out of his nose.' He bursts out in laughter.

'We're eating, man,' Kieran says, but he puts down the garlic bread to watch the video instead.

My phone vibrates in my pocket.

Mum's calling.

'It's my mum. She's probably calling about the drone,' I say excitedly to my friends, and answer, 'Hi, Mum.'

'Happy birthday to you! Happy birthday to you! Happy birthday to Isaiah. Happy birthday to you,' she sings through the phone. *'What's that racket in the background?'*

'Thanks, Mum. I'm at Fucchinis with Kieran, Kieran's mum and Fredrick.'

'Shouldn't your father be there with you? Never mind. Sorry I couldn't call you earlier, class ran over. And about your present . . .'

'I can't wait for the drone to get here.' My friends hear that, bumping each other.

'I know I promised, but I won't be able to get it right now because of how tight things are here. You know I'm a student again and I only work part time.'

I move away from the table.

I want to tell her how *bad* things are for Dad and me, but I don't because Dad would hate me telling.

'I knew a smart boy like you would understand,' Mum says.

'I understand.' *But I don't.*

Chapter Four

Tuesday

Before I leave for school, I rummage through the kitchen drawer for the heated pads. Dad's bundled up in layers on the sofa as the cold affects his body. I tuck the warm pads around him.

'Thanks, Isaiah,' Dad murmurs, his eyes tracking me in the dark room. 'I'm sorry for ruining your birthday. I'll make it up to you, promise.'

'It's all right, Dad. You didn't ruin it,' I reply. 'See you after school.'

Mr Paterson, my history teacher, stands on the table and hops on one leg. He does strange things like this all the time, but he's been the best teacher in this school so far.

'Now that I've got your attention,' he says. 'As you know, I've been monitoring your work this term on nineteenth century Britain. If you have forgotten, the student or students who have made the best attempt at homework, class participation and overall grades will be representing the school at the Victorian exhibition in a few weeks with a cash prize for the winners of £250. I will be approaching the students this week about it.'

'I can get another pair of Jordans with that money,' I comment, thinking about the ones Uncle Kwame got me.

'Not if Mr Paterson chooses *me* for the exhibition and *I* win,' Fredrick says.

'We're going to do a quick starter on what we've learnt on the Industrial Revolution thus far and *then* we're going to dive . . .' Mr Paterson springs off the table, landing squarely in his suede boots that he wears most days. '. . . into the impact of it.'

'Isaiah, has the drone come yet?' Kieran asks.

Luckily, when the pizza arrived at our table yesterday, they were too distracted to ask about the drone. Fredrick also tried to eat three pizza slices at once. I've been bragging about the drone for weeks and now I don't know if I'm going to even get it. Anger sparks inside like a firework. *My friends won't understand if I tell them.* Kieran's family is loaded and Fredrick's brothers buy him stuff all the time.

'Stop keeping us in suspense, man,' Fredrick says, rubbing his hands together. 'Where's the drone? Is it in your bag?'

'It hasn't come yet. It's stuck in the airport,' I reply,

thinking of more things to tell them. 'You know it's coming from Berlin.'

'And as you know the Industrial Revolution happened last year . . . or was that when I got my last haircut?' Mr Paterson remarks, running his fingers through his straggly brown locks. 'Who knows. In pairs, you'll be designing a poster, nothing fancy, to show an area of change during the Industrial Revolution. Partner with a person whose surname starts with the same letter as yours. Go.'

'Are you coming over later to play *FIFA*?' Kieran asks.

Tuesdays are food bank days. Since Dad isn't feeling well, I have to go there to get our weekly shopping. It's the worst bit of my day.

I shake my head.

'Why don't we go cinema this weekend then? I wanna watch that film. What's the name again?'

Fredrick is always forgetting something. A name. His lunch. He forgot his shoes once.

I think. 'It must be the new Legend film! *The Return of the Legend.*'

'Yeah, that's it.' Fredrick snaps his fingers together. 'Do you wanna go then? There's a twelve o'clock showing – my sister can get us a discount.'

If I had money, I could say yes to everything, but I don't and I'm *not* asking my friends for it.

'That doesn't sound like talk on the Industrial

Revolution,' Mr Paterson jokes. 'Happy belated birthday, Isaiah, and merry Christmas to you all.'

Fredrick's in stitches. 'Sir, Christmas was months ago. Did you forget?'

'Oh really? I must've woken up on the wrong side of the bed.' Mr Paterson turns to me. 'If I remember correctly, Isaiah, only you and Kesia have surnames beginning with "O". Young Kesia over there is probably wondering why you won't design a lovely poster with her.' He moves on to another desk.

Fredrick's and Kieran's surnames both start with an 'A' so they get to work together while I drag my feet over to Kesia's desk. There's nothing *really* so bad about Kesia, but we don't talk – even when I see her around my block of flats.

'You've started,' I say, sitting down as Kesia draws a title.

'Only a bit. You were taking too long,' she replies, and tightens the band holding her afro puff. 'We can do the poster on technology and transport during the Industrial Revolution. I know you like tech.'

'How do you know that?' I ask.

Kesia looks at me funny. 'Because we've been in the same class for a year and we live in the same block of flats. I see you taking books out in the library too.'

I *do* have a book on inventions in my bag.

25

Kesia focuses on the poster again. 'You come up with some facts to add to the poster and I'll design. What do you want to start with?'

'Okaaay. Let's start with steam trains . . .'

'What have you got for me?' Mr Paterson sings, and points his clicker at the SMART Board. 'Yes, Isaiah.'

'Technology and transport,' I answer.

'What about it?'

'Steam trains. They could transport items and more people could travel.'

'Bingo!' Mr Paterson claps. 'Steam trains transformed it all. George Stephenson and Isambard Kingdom Brunel oversaw the "railway mania" of the eighteen hundreds. Hit me with something again. Kevin?'

Kevin gives an answer about people moving to cities.

'Yes. Correct. Hundreds of thousands of families left the countryside and moved to new but often cramped houses in the rapidly expanding cities.

'While the Industrial Revolution was indeed revolutionary, it had *huge* social costs, i.e. the dehumanisation of workers, child labour, pollution, and the growth of cities where poverty, filth and disease flourished. We're going to watch a short video clip now which shows the reality of how the poor and homeless lived, in particular those living in workhouses. Victorian workhouses housed

26

orphans, the sick, the disabled, the elderly and unmarried mothers too.'

Mr Paterson plays a grainy black-and-white video. Kids with shaved heads stand outside in thick corduroy trousers, grey flannel shirts, black jackets, hats, and boots. Some of them must be around my age.

'Our own town, Shepten, nearly went bankrupt in the mid-nineteenth century, but a local benefactor, Madame Rosalind Danvers, rescued it. She owned the town for many years, making changes to Shepten that you still see today, like building the clock tower on top of the library. Can anyone guess what our school building used to be? Yes, Kesia.'

'It used to be Shepten Hospital.'

People around the room start to whisper. An unexpected shiver runs through me and it's as if I hear the clock tower bells chiming in my head. *Ding. Ding. Ding.*

After school, I shoulder the heavy parcel from the food bank, stopping by the big black bins at the bottom of our flats to adjust the load.

There's a door by the bins leading down to the basement. I've never been down there before. Fredrick dared Kieran to go in once, but Kieran was too scared and Fredrick was too. *I'm not.*

The ground slopes down and my shoes hit the cement as I tread deeper, using the torch from my phone. The light reflects off the large, dusty, abandoned room with brick walls and grimy square windows that have been boarded up. Tucked in the corner of the room is an old grimy fireplace. I take a photo of it and then film myself.

'Kieran, Fredrick. Guess where I am?' I flip the camera round to record the room. 'I'm in that abandoned basement in my flats that you both were scared of.' I sneeze. 'It's dusty.'

I stop recording, putting the phone back in my pocket. The birthday card from Mum falls out of my hoodie.

'I know I promised, but I won't be able to get it right now . . .'

Without thinking, I scrunch up the card and throw it inside the old fireplace. There's a whoosh and suddenly it bursts to life with a green-coloured flame.

'What the . . .' I jump back, shielding my face in case it explodes but nothing else happens. *Why is the flame green? Was it because of the card?*

I creep back towards the fireplace. After a few seconds, the flame dies down and I get an idea for a little experiment.

I shrug my hood back and run up the basement slope, heading back towards the big black bins. The smell carries its way right up my nose. Bracing myself against the bins, I push my body up, hovering over the top to grab pieces of rubbish.

Running back to the fireplace, I throw some greasy chip-shop paper inside. The flames spark and they change to red. I was right! The colour changes depending on what I throw inside.

'This is so cool.' I flip my phone to selfie mode and spin round so the fire is my backdrop. A message comes through from Dad asking where I am, but I ignore it. The flames spark again, leaping higher and making me jump forward.

Then, through the hazy flames reflected over my shoulder, the back of the fireplace reveals a thin light-skinned boy around my age with a shaved head. His body flickers like the flames. *Whaaaaaaat?! This can't be real.*

Ding. Ding. Ding.

I drop my phone and scrabble around in the dust for it. Spinning round to the fireplace, I quickly try to take a picture, but, when I look at my screen, it's just a weird blur.

The fire disappears and the boy with it.

That's when I notice it. A shiny object is left behind in the fireplace. I pick it up, dusting off the ash. It's a fancy gold fountain pen. It definitely wasn't in there before.

I roll the pen between my fingers, noticing curly looping engravings on it.

Jacob Ephraim Akintola.

Chapter Five

Wednesday

Dad crunches on his Coco Pops, happy that we have something other than oats to eat this week.

I google on my phone and write on my whiteboard. Making lists is the only way I can get things straight in my head sometimes. When you're fixing things, there's a process you kind of have to follow. It's like that, I guess.

'What are you researching?' he asks between mouthfuls.

'History.'

What did the Perryville Estate flats in Shepten used to be? Cricklewood Workhouse.

Why could I see that boy in the fireplace? Tiredness.

It's the *only* reason. But then how do I explain the fountain pen in my pocket?

'What's got you concentrating so hard?' Dad asks. 'And thanks for getting the groceries from the food bank. I'm feeling better today.'

'It's all right,' I mumble.

<u>Ghosts aren't real!!</u>

I underline it twice because ghosts don't exist and I don't believe in them. Wasn't it Albert Einstein who said *The important thing is not to stop questioning*?

Ding. Ding. Ding.

The clock chimes in my head, reminding me of Mr Paterson's history lesson yesterday and that video of the workhouse.

Dad drinks the remaining chocolate milk in his bowl, wiping away the droplets on his chin. 'Where are you rushing off to?'

'School!' I shout.

I arrive at the gates with one mission: find Mr Paterson, but it's not as easy as I thought. He's not in any of the classrooms, in the canteen or out by the fields. I keep on missing him.

'There he is,' Fredrick says, pointing at our history teacher coming towards us in the corridor. He's surrounded by a group of teachers and sipping coffee from a personalised ancient-history mug. *Have people always put their names on things?*

I touch my pocket, feeling the fireplace pen still there. It's my only proof that I wasn't seeing things.

'Mr Paterson!' I shout down the corridor, and once he

sees me he ducks, hiding behind another teacher.

My friends laugh. I leave them to go speak with Mr Paterson, who looks down at me with a grin. He *always* smells of coffee and mint.

'Sir, I was calling you.'

'Were you? I swear on my dear mother's life that I had no idea. Do you think a respectable teacher such as myself would run away when a student is in need?'

'You're not funny, sir.'

Tilting his nose up at me, Mr Paterson responds. 'My theatre group would say otherwise. How may I be of assistance, my twentieth favourite student?'

'It's about that video you showed us last lesson. Where did you get it from?'

'Now, Isaiah,' Mr Paterson says. 'I can't reveal my sources – YouTube. I got the video from YouTube,' he whispers, 'but don't tell the other students. It's a secret.' Mr Paterson puts a finger to his chapped lips.

'There aren't any workhouses now . . . are there?' I ask, picturing the boy in the flames.

'No.' He taps his suede boots together, smacking his lips as he chews on his mint gum. 'The Local Government Act of 1929 abolished workhouses. However, the workhouse buildings are still in use today, but for different purposes.'

'My block of flats used to be Cricklewood Workhouse.'

I take out my phone, showing him the picture I took of the strange fireplace.

Mr Paterson whistles. 'It has all its original mouldings. Spectacular. The past is still very much present, Isaiah. Even when we don't want it to, the past has a *profound* impact on our future.'

My body tenses.

I know that without Dad's accident we wouldn't have lost our house and moved to Shepten.

Suddenly the colour in the corridor changes. It's grainy and flickering black and white like the workhouse video. The corridor is missing lockers. Through the classroom window by us, the chairs and tables have been replaced with hospital beds. In another second, everything is back to normal.

The bell rings and people speed around me, but I feel like I'm stuck. *What was that?*

'And that is my cue to skedaddle,' Mr Paterson says. 'Always a pleasure discussing history with you, Isaiah. And if you ever want to know more, you can ask me or, better still, visit the public library. It's packed full of Shepten's history. I've got to go.'

I feel the pen in my pocket again. 'Wait. What about if I want to find info on someone from the past?'

'Google the National Archives. I really have to go or my class will eat each other alive. They're like rabid wolves.'

'What were you talking to Mr Paterson about?' Kieran asks, appearing beside me with Fredrick on my other side.

'I need to go to the library really quick,' I reply, still not believing what I saw.

There's not much to the library at school. It's tiny, but they have the best books. When it was winter, I'd sometimes get my friends to stay with me here until it closed. I could read and keep warm because the flat wasn't, but I didn't tell them that.

I leave Kieran and Fredrick in the comics section.

'I've added a new book on engineering to your shelf, Isaiah,' Nancy, the school librarian, says. She reminds me of a spider with her round middle, spindly legs and jet-black hair.

'Thanks, Nancy,' I reply, pulling out the chair at the last free computer. 'I'm doing history research.'

I've never been into *other* parts of history except facts on inventions or anything to do with technology.

'I love to hear that you're branching out,' Nancy says. 'Shout if you need help.'

I take the fountain pen out of my pocket and type *Jacob Ephraim Akintola* into the National Archives.

I don't realise Kesia's sitting next to me until she leans back in her chair, clearing her throat. 'What are you searching? Is that for history?'

I turn the computer screen so she can't see what I'm doing. 'No.'

I click the search result at the top.

CRICKLEWOOD WORKHOUSE ADMISSIONS
This record is held by London Archives.
Name: Jacob Ephraim Akintola
Age: 13 years old

Date of death: UNKNOWN/UNRECORDED

Chapter Six

We're laughing as we cross the road to walk home after school.

'You'd better come over to mine later,' Kieran says. 'We haven't been over in time. Isaiah, what's your dad doing here?' He points across the road.

'I dunno, but I'll chat to you later.' I stick my fist out, bumping with Kieran and Fredrick.

'Laters,' they say.

'I thought I'd come and pick you up,' Dad answers the question in my head as I stop in front of him.

'Why today?' I ask. 'I'm old enough to go home by myself.'

'Yes, I know you're a big man,' Dad replies, reaching his hand out to tug on my braids, but I duck him. Laughing, Dad straightens and clears his throat. 'I wanted to come and meet you because I've got some good news. I got the job.'

'I *knew* you would get it.'

We cross another road. I slow down, so Dad can catch up.

'This could be the beginning of great things,' he says, holding on to my shoulder. 'Do you hear me, son? Great things for both of us.'

My phone vibrates and Mum's name pops up on the screen. I've been ignoring her since my birthday, but I know she'll keep calling. This is the longest I've gone without speaking to her and it's only been two days.

'What did your mother do now?' Dad asks, watching me ignore the call. 'Did she at least apologise for calling you late on your birthday?' Dad fidgets, clearing his throat. 'I feel like we both let you down. I know you wanted a proper tablet for your birthday, not a whiteboard.'

'Yeah, she *did* say sorry,' I reply. 'And I like the whiteboard. Everyone has a tablet, but having a whiteboard is kinda original.'

Dad grumbles, complaining to himself about Mum. We get home, but our front door is wide open. Dad pushes the door open further with his hand. 'Isaiah, wait here.'

Shouting erupts from inside the flat and a random couple rush out the door seconds later.

'Dad!' I call, going in.

Dad holds his back with one hand while advancing towards our landlord with a pinched expression as he takes in long breaths. 'You're supposed to give us warning before you have people viewing the flat.'

Our landlord stands opposite Dad in a mismatched suit. He still straightens the jacket like he's important.

'I'll get that possession order any day now!' he seethes. 'You're lucky I haven't kicked you out on the street already, missing all those payments.'

'Missed payments,' I say, drawing all the attention to me. 'What payments? My dad hasn't missed any payments!'

Because if he did, he would've said so.

The landlord laughs. 'Setting a good example for your son, are you? Keeping things from him. Keeping my rent money.'

'Don't bring my son into this!' Dad shouts, and drops his hand from his back, trying to straighten his posture. 'I *never* lied to him.'

Yeah, he just didn't tell me he missed any rent payments.

'And you've always had it in for me . . . for us! You never fix anything that needs to be fixed in this building. Even after I explained my *situation* to you.'

The landlord scoffs. 'Yes, we all have problems. I'm not giving you any more chances.'

'You expect me to pay for this place when it's falling apart!'

'Expect a letter from the court.' The landlord leaves the flat and I follow, hurrying behind him down the stairs.

'Can't you give my dad more time?' I ask, remembering how long it took us to find this place. 'He's just got a new job. It's not fair!'

'Life's not fair,' he remarks.

'Isn't there something my dad can do?' I ask, jumping in front of him and blocking the exit.

'There *is* something your dad can do.' Hope builds in my chest, but then it's crushed like an old Coke can. 'He can start by paying off five hundred pounds. If he can get me that money by the end of the month, then *maybe* I'll pause the eviction.'

Eviction.

The end of the month is only two weeks from today. Our landlord drives off, leaving me here wondering what we're gonna do.

Ding. Ding. Ding.

The public library at the end of my street changes and begins to flicker like the school corridor did. The rest of the street is normal, but the library is grainy and has no colour, shaky like those old-timey films. The clock on top of the library chimes three more times.

Ding. Ding. Ding.

Chapter Seven

I enter the basement, ready to get answers somehow. Ever since I watched that video in history, everything has been strange. Is Mr Paterson testing me? Is this some kind of weird prank?

The dusty fireplace is exactly how it was last time. 'Where are you hiding the camera, Mr Paterson?'

I feel around the mantel for anything; black soot coats my fingertips. I leave the basement to get some rubbish to start a new fire.

Bracing myself against the black bins, I push myself up, hovering over the top to pick up some old newspapers.

I head straight for the fireplace, tossing the rubbish inside. After a few seconds, the strange blue flames burst into life, but this time they have a yellow tinge to them.

'Hello!' I shout. 'Where are you? I know you're there!'

I wait for the fireplace to shift and reveal the boy that

I *think* I saw. The flame just keeps burning, but the boy doesn't appear.

Eventually the fire dies down, burning down enough for me to see a torn piece of newspaper left in the fireplace.

THE ILLUSTRATED POLICE CHRONICLE
LAW-COURTS AND WEEKLY RECORD
SHEPTEN, MARCH 17, 1838.

Is this a joke newspaper? Why isn't it burnt?

ANOTHER DEATH FROM STARVATION
IN SHEPTEN

On Monday, Dr Latimore held an inquest at the St. Marylebone workhouse investigating the death of Mary Lucas, who died suddenly last Friday. Mary, who was 46 years old, had been ill for a considerable time from an unknown disease. She had lived in the front kitchen near the workhouse with her brother. They paid 2s. 6d. per week. The deceased only had 3s. 6d. per week from the parish. She had no other relief. The doctor had only seen her after she had passed. A witness believed she died from the want of nourishment. She had wished Mary to go into the workhouse but the deceased refused to go. The coroner could not understand how either of them could live upon the miserable sum of money they received.

Scrawled at the back of the torn newspaper is a letter written in the neatest handwriting I've ever seen.

Dear boy with the braided hair,
It's a pleasure to make your acquaintance. I left this letter perchance we see each other again.

Is he talking about me? Am I the boy with braided hair?

My name is Jacob Ephraim Akintola, and misfortune has befallen me.

The pen belongs to him!

I've been abandoned by my uncle Francis at this dreadful workhouse. He promised that I would only be here for a short while, but it's been weeks and I haven't heard a word from him. When I arrived here, they stripped me of all my belongings like they do common thieves. I'm forced to wear this horrid uniform that itches, sleep by hundreds of other boys and eat slop that is unfit for a dog. Am I not worth more than a dog?

The workhouse guardian, Mr Moore, despises me for my upbringing. He has threatened multiple times to cast me out if I don't pull my weight but I'm struggling with the tasks. Oakum picking for hours has created tiny cuts in my palms that sting when water touches them.

Uncle Francis tells me my father is dead and, as an orphan, that's why I'm here. My father went on one of his regular business trips to Lagos, Nigeria, and he hasn't been heard from since. I'm worried that something has happened to him. And I know that he would never have left me in a place like this. The children here are apathetic at best, but you must have extraordinary powers of intelligence if you are able to see me through a fireplace. I must leave this place immediately. I require your assistance.

Yours faithfully,
Jacob

My head feels like it's going to explode. Jacob is real. He's real and he's trapped in Cricklewood Workhouse. I couldn't imagine Uncle Kwame leaving me somewhere like that.

My phone pings.

Kieran: where r u?

Mum: please answer my calls
I'm so sorry about your birthday.
I know I promised.
I can't have you upset with me

Dad is calling

I run up the stairs, away from the basement and Jacob. Away from everything that's making my head spin.

'Come on, Garrett Morgan, we're almost there,' a Black woman with bantu knots and dungarees splattered with paint says to a white rabbit that's hopping up the concrete steps beside her.

'Garrett Morgan the inventor of traffic lights . . . that Garrett Morgan?' I ask.

The woman turns round on the stairs to face me. 'I'm a fan of *anyone* who knows G.M.' She offers her free hand to shake. 'Clarice. What's your name?'

'Isaiah,' I reply.

Clarice moves around a stack of cardboard boxes at the top of the stairs. I point to them. 'Are you moving into the flat on the top floor?'

'Yes, I am. I'm guessing you live here too.'

My phone beeps with another call from Dad coming through.

'Middle floor. I've gotta go.'

'I will see you around, Isaiah.'

As soon as I get into the flat, Dad gets me to repeat everything the landlord said.

'Is that all he said?' Dad quizzes me with a thoughtful look on his face like he's working things out in his head.

'Something about eviction.'

'We're not going anywhere!' Dad thunders. 'I *know* the law like the back of my hand. And if he tries, I will fight him. He can't kick us out of our home.'

'What are we gonna do if he does?' I ask.

Dad laughs like I've told the funniest joke. 'And who else will put up with him? You can't believe his bluff.'

'I can help raise the money or we can ask Mum.'

Dad frowns, rubbing at a sore spot on his back. 'Your mother is off studying and living her dreams. She can't help us. I don't want you to worry, Isaiah. I put too much on you as it is. This will work itself out, you'll see. I've got my new job now; it should be enough. But if I do take on odd jobs, you can tag along as my partner. It'll be like old times.'

It'll be *nothing* like old times because everything is different.

Chapter Eight

Thursday

Mum: Are you still ignoring me?

> **Me:** ~~dad owes money~~
> ~~we're getting kicked out~~
> No

I can't still be angry over a stupid drone when we could be kicked out of our home, but I am.

'Can everyone gather around the front desk?' Mrs Coleman, our science teacher, says. I pocket my phone before she sees. 'One slice of apple was covered with vinegar, one with lemon juice and one with salt water. Can you check if your hypotheses were correct about the apple slices? What did you predict would happen to each slice?'

Discreetly, I take the whiteboard out of my bag. Everyone surrounds Mrs Coleman as we check our predictions for the apple experiment, but I'm not listening.

Hypothesis about Jacob

Old hypothesis – ~~Jacob isn't real because ghosts~~
~~don't exist and Mr Paterson is pulling a prank on me.~~

New hypothesis – Jacob is real and I'm not
seeing a ghost. I can see Jacob because he lived
in the workhouse which used to be my flat.

And I brainstorm some more in the history lesson when I'm supposed to be listening to Mr Paterson.

Am I the only one who can see Jacob? Can
other people on my estate see him too?

'*Isaiah.*' I hear a faint crackly voice.

'Yeah?' I answer back, looking around to see who's calling out. 'Kieran, did you say something?'

'Did I say something?' Kieran repeats, watching me. 'No. Are you hearing things?'

If Kieran didn't call my name, who did?

'And how comes you didn't come over yesterday? Fredrick scored an own goal.'

Should I tell Kieran about Jacob? Will he believe me?

'Kieran—'

'What are you talking about?' Fredrick whispers, butting into the conversation.

'Nothing.'

'We've looked at what the Industrial Revolution was, but today we're going to look at who it benefitted,' Mr Paterson says. 'Feast your eyes on this short video about the upper class, the middle class and the working class. Hands up if you've heard these terms before.'

A few people raise their hands. 'I would've been part of the upper class. You can see from my expensive attire.' Mr Paterson pokes his finger through the hole in his blazer pocket and a few people laugh.

'In groups of four or five,' Mr Paterson says after the video ends, 'you'll receive a set of statements. Read each statement and the group can decide which of the three social classes it best matches. Off you go.'

Kieran, Fredrick, Kirsty, Kesia and I are all put together. Fredrick can't keep the smile off his face at having Kirsty in our group.

'I'll read the first one,' Kirsty offers. '*My cotton factory might as well be printing money. The huge demand, new technology, and cheap child labour means I'm rich.*'

'Upper class,' Kesia replies without waiting for the question.

'Okaaaay.' When Kesia's head is bent writing, Kirsty

mouths something over her. Fredrick laughs.

'What's the next statement?' I ask Kirsty.

'*I'm only eleven yet work down the coal mine from five a.m. to five p.m. I spend most of the time stood in water, hardly ever see daylight and am badly treated.*'

'It must be working class,' I answer.

'I'll do the next one,' Kieran says. '*I'm glad I became a clerk. With all these new industries needing bookkeeping, I'm never short of work . . .*'

'Spectacular work today, class. How great am I at my job?' Mr Paterson asks, and there's grumbling around the room. 'OK, OK. I get it. Your homework. I want you to note down some of the positive and negative effects of the Industrial Revolution for all social classes. Now scram, you eager beavers.'

I wait behind a second for Kesia. I wonder if she's seen anything strange in the building before.

'Have you ever been down to the basement of our flats?' I ask.

'No, why? What's down there?' she asks.

'There's this old fireplace.' I slowly take out the newspaper clipping. 'You're sure? You've never seen anything weird at all?'

'I'm sure. What's that? Can I see?'

'Yeah.'

Kesia plucks the newspaper out of my hand, examining

the article. 'Wow, is this an original Victorian newspaper clipping?'

I can't properly focus on all Kesia's questions because she's about to turn it over and see the letter Jacob wrote to me. I snatch it back.

'Why did you snatch it?' Kesia sulks. 'I thought you said I could look.'

'I changed my mind.'

'Whatever, Isaiah.' She leaves the classroom and Mr Paterson comes over.

'Did my ears hear correctly? An *original* Victorian newspaper clipping? Your research must be going well.'

'Yeah, kinda, but . . . I'll figure it out.'

'Yes, keep that confidence because I have some good news for you.' Mr Paterson pauses. 'You're one of the students who'll be representing the school for the Victorian exhibition – if you accept. Students from each school must give a presentation on the theme of the exhibition: our connections with the past. It would mean researching outside of lessons, but you'd have support from me too. Alongside the £250 cash prize, the winners will get private viewing access to an exhibition of their choice with extra tickets free for friends and family. I want you to consider representing the school, Isaiah.'

Chapter Nine

'Isaiah, where are you going?' Kieran asks as I split off from them down the road. 'Aren't you coming round any more?'

'I can't today cos—'

'Mum is gonna order us takeaway tonight.'

'I'll see if I can come over. You know my dad might not let me out,' I lie because Dad *would* let me. 'Laters.' I leave before they ask me something else.

'Why is he acting funny?' I hear Fredrick mutter to Kieran.

I ignore him and race down the road towards our flats. My phones vibrates in my pocket. I answer it.

'Hi, Mum. I can't talk.'

She sighs. *'Why not? I thought you'd forgiven me for the whole birthday situation. Put your video on. Let me see your face.'*

I fumble with the phone. 'Mum, it's not that. I've just gotta go somewhere.'

'Where? You can't talk to your own mother for five minutes when she doesn't get to speak to you much as it is.'

'It's not my fault you moved,' I mumble, hoping she doesn't hear, but she does.

'You know this architecture programme is a great opportunity for me.' Mum's voice rises. 'I'm sorry I can't be there for you all the time, but I promised I'd make it up to you. I said I'd try to come and visit in a few months. Don't you want me to follow my dreams? You know I've always wanted to study again.'

'I get it,' I reply, remembering what Mr Paterson said. 'I've got news too. My history teacher asked me to represent the school for this Victorian exhibition.'

'That is incredible, Isaiah, well done! Of course your teacher would ask you to represent the school. Look at both of us doing new and exciting things.'

'The exhibition is in three weeks. The winner gets tickets for their family to go to a private exhibition that we get to choose. You can come for that.'

Mum laughs. 'Always so confident. I would love to come . . . but with school and the job, it's too tight.'

The clock tower chimes ring out. 'Mum. I've gotta go.'

'Fine. I'll see what I can do, Isaiah.' Mum takes in a deep breath, rubbing her forehead. 'Bye, son.'

'Thanks, Mum!'

Leaning over the bin, I snatch a discarded stack of club flyers and rush into the basement. 'This better work.'

I throw the flyers into the fireplace. The fire splutters for a second, but nothing happens.

I wait some more and still the fire continues to burn without Jacob appearing. I take the fountain pen out of my pocket, rolling it between my fingers.

'Oh, thank heavens you're here again!' Jacob cries out, and I almost jump in surprise at hearing his voice. *'You weren't a hallucination.'*

'My theory was right,' I whisper to myself. I can speak to someone from the past! 'This is weird.'

I pace in front of the fireplace, trying to make sense of what's happening. 'What's the broom for?'

'I sweep the fireplaces as part of my work every two days.' Jacob leans on the broom, peering through the fire. *'What is this you're wearing?'*

'This?' I say, pinching the school jumper between my fingers. 'It's my school uniform. Don't you go to school?'

'There are classes at Cricklewood, but I wouldn't call it that when we don't have the proper tools.' Jacob sulks. *'I was tutored at home before this by the governess, who also taught my mother, which her family hated. When it was time for me to go to boarding school, Mother passed away, so Father insisted I remain at home.'*

'I'm sorry about your mum.'

'What is a "mum"?' he asks, confused. *Are you from London? You speak rather peculiarly.*

I laugh. 'No, it's you who talks posh.' I take out Jacob's creased letter from my pocket. 'The newspaper article you wrote your letter on says the year is 1838. It's around the same date here, but the year is 2023.'

Fiddlesticks! If you're from the year 2023 as you say, then time travel truly does exist! My goodness. Jacob taps his broom on the floor twice.

I burst out laughing. 'There's no time travel – only in films at the cinema.'

Oh, what is a "cinema"?

'You don't know what a cinema is? It's place where you go to watch films . . . you know . . . on screens. Don't you have films there? You watch actors on the screen. Don't tell me you *don't* have actors?'

Jacob looks confused. *Father and I used to watch performances at the theatre, but not through a screen. Why are the performers behind a screen?*

'Let me show you.' I hold up my phone and search for cinemas on Google.

Jacob jumps back. *Sorcery! How extraordinary. You have powers untold and must help me. I need to find my father and leave this despicable place.*

I hold up the newspaper article again and ask,

'Do people really die because they don't have enough food?'

'Indeed. I was raised in privilege thus shielded from it all, but not here — not at Cricklewood.'

Sometimes Dad and I struggle, but I can't believe people died in Shepten because they didn't have enough food. 'How did you end up at Cricklewood?'

'It all began a few weeks ago.' As Jacob starts talking, the fireplace changes, flickering black and white.

I can see the inside of a mansion with the longest hallways and red carpets, large bedrooms and a wide porch. There are suitcases stacked on top of each other.

'My uncle paid people to pack my belongings away in trunks. I never saw my things again. My childhood home. Gone.'

An older woman in a white apron with red cheeks crushes Jacob into a hug, messing up his neatly combed curls.

'It's not right what they're doing to you, master Jacob,' the woman cries.

'Grace had helped raise me. My uncle refused to explain where he was taking me to.'

Jacob and his uncle get into a horse-drawn carriage and they leave the mansion behind. The horses speed away down the cobbled streets. They stop outside a large stone building with many windows. *My estate!*

The brand-new clock tower at the end of the street

chimes three times and the fireplace turns back to normal.

'And that's how I ended up here,' Jacob explains. *'But I still don't understand why. If he had indeed passed away, my father would've put measures in place to ensure I was well taken care of. I know he has a will.'*

'Why would your own uncle do something like that?' I ask, confused and angry for Jacob. 'My uncle Kwame would never.'

'Then he's a much finer man than my uncle Francis and he calls himself a nobleman. I should have known something wasn't right because I barely knew my uncle. He never really came to visit me. My mother's family liked to pretend my father and I didn't exist.'

'Why not?'

'They didn't approve of my parents' union. A marriage between a white woman of rank and a Black man was unheard of – even though my father was very *successful. I preferred it when it just us three.'*

I did too. Dad, Mum and I.

'What do you say?' Jacob asks. *'Will you help me locate my father? Can you find his will? If it's a financial concern, you'll be well compensated for your help once I am rightly restored to my former position.'*

The fire burns fiercer as I spit back, 'It's *not* about the money.' I think about me being separated from my dad. I think about what would happen to me if he wasn't around any more. And then I think about how it *is* about the money, the rent that we need to pay back our landlord . . . And that gives me an idea.

'I'll help you find your dad, but I need your help too. I need you to tell me everything you know about Shepten in the past . . . what it's really like to live there, first-hand. Stuff I can't find out anywhere else.'

'Yes, yes. I'll help you with anything as long as it gets me out of this filthy place and back with my father.'

'We have a deal then?'

The flame flickers. *'What name do you go by?'*

'My name's Isaiah.'

Chapter Ten

When I got home, Dad told me to get ready because we were going out. He hasn't told me where yet.

Dad whistles as people rush past us on the high street. 'Do you remember when you used to follow me around with your fake toolbox? Your stubby little legs wanting to help me fix things around the house?'

'My legs weren't stubby!'

'And your nappy would sometimes be full, so you'd run with your bum sticking out like a bee.' Dad's hip stiffly jerks from side to side as he tries to imitate toddler-me running.

'No, I didn't!' I laugh. 'I didn't run like that.'

'I'm going to do those odd jobs to raise some more money,' Dad says, squinting. 'You can be my little helper again.'

'What about your back? You're not supposed—'

'My back should hold. What do I always say when people say you can't do something?'

'You *can* do it. You *can* do anything and everything,' I respond.

'There we go, so don't worry about me,' Dad says. 'I'll be just fine.'

I swallow down the crashing waves in my stomach. He's right. We *can* do anything.

'How's IT going this year?' Dad asks. 'You explained to your class how computers are made yet?'

I laugh. 'Not yet, but I should. And IT is all right,' I say, explaining about our website project. 'Though I'm not sure what business I should do.'

'I know you'll come up with something good. What about your other subjects?'

'I'm into all kinds of things now, like history.'

'History?' Dad chuckles. 'Since when?'

Since I started seeing and talking to a Victorian boy in a fireplace!

'My teacher asked if I could represent the school for this Victorian exhibition we're going to. Once we win, we get to go to this private exhibition with our family and friends and . . . And that sort of thing.'

Dad clasps me on the shoulder. 'You and your big brains.'

More like me and my big mouth. Can't believe I nearly told him about the prize money. I can't get his hopes up like that. But I do need to win. I have to.

'Do you believe in ghosts, Dad?'

'Where did that come from?' he asks, staring at me. 'I'm not sure about ghosts *per se*, but I do believe that we're not alone here.'

I pause on the spot outside Uncle Kwame's barbershop. 'Really?'

Dad nods.

'What would you do if someone . . . from the past came to you?'

'I doubt that would ever happen, but if it did, I'd ask what they wanted,' Dad replies. 'You don't have an encounter for no reason.'

Uncle Kwame knocks on his shop window, catching our attention. He steps on to the street with an old toolbox.

'Here you go, brother,' Uncle says to Dad, handing him the toolbox. 'It was just collecting dust at the back of the shop.'

I forgot that Dad had to sell his expensive tools after he got injured at work. We needed money for things around the house. Dad *loved* his tools.

'Thanks, Kwame.'

Uncle Kwame strokes his salt and pepper hair. 'It's good you're helping your dad out, young blood. I used to help my old man when I was about your age too. I stayed out of trouble.'

'Isaiah is too smart to get himself in trouble,' Dad replies. 'Thanks again.'

We turn off the cobbled streets, stopping outside the house on the left. Dad knocks and a slim woman with thinning brown hair opens the door. She's carrying a screaming baby with dark spikes of hair stuck to her forehead.

'Andrea?' Dad asks. 'I'm here to fix some furniture.'

'Finally,' she breathes, before nodding her head at me. 'What is he doing here? I'm not running a daycare.'

'My son is here to assist; he's very capable – top of his class. Which room is the furniture being fitted in?'

Her voice is clipped as she beckons us into the tight hallway. 'Fine, but I'm not responsible for him.'

A little boy with a crusty nose pulls at my leg, getting my attention. He points at the fizzy TV.

'Do you want me to fix it for you?' I ask, moving towards it.

I fiddle with the cables at the back and the TV flashes back to life. The boy claps.

'Isaiah, I need your help here,' Dad calls from the hallway.

'We've decided that the office will be up in the attic instead,' the woman says. 'Is that going to be a problem?' She shoves a slice of apple into the baby's mouth to keep her quiet. 'Because your ad said you do *all* fittings regardless of the location of the house. If money is an issue, my husband can pay more.'

Speaking through his teeth, Dad responds, 'I can do it. No problem.'

'Great,' she replies. 'Would you mind carrying the box up the stairs? It's only a small one. I hope you don't mind.'

The woman climbs the stairs with the baby tucked into her hip.

'I'll lift from the bottom,' I say to Dad. With the weight and motion, I'll be carrying most of the weight from below, so it doesn't hurt his back as much.

'Thanks, son,' he whispers, readying himself to lift. 'One, two, three, lift.'

I do what Dad says, heaving the box up the first flight of stairs and then to the attic. Dad's face pinches. Pain is an extra layer of skin for him now.

'I'll take the things out of the box,' I say quietly.

Chapter Eleven

Friday

The morning comes quickly, the cold creeping through my thin bedsheets as I prep the used iPad case someone threw away and I brought home. The case is worn and has scratches, but after measuring the whiteboard, it's just about the same dimensions.

Using the retractable knife from Uncle Kwame's toolbox, I carefully cut slits in all four corners, so when I slip the whiteboard in, the edges poke out of the sides. It's not perfect, but I can carry it around more easily and the cover will prevent any smudging too.

'Agggggh!' I hear Dad's scream.

I jump out of bed, calling for Dad as I run down the corridor towards the sofa. 'Dad?'

'Isaiah, I can't move,' he strains, forcing the words out between his teeth. 'My back.'

I *knew* Dad shouldn't have been doing all that heavy lifting yesterday, but he wouldn't listen to me.

'Do you need help getting comfortable?'

Dad nods and points at his special back support pillow that has fallen on the floor. I pick it up and slot it behind him. He gives me a thumbs up.

'I'll see if we have any more painkillers.' The cold tiles in the kitchen freeze my bare feet as I check under the sink, finding only an empty packet.

7:45.

'All the painkillers are done, Dad. I'm going to the pharmacy to pick up some more. I've got your prescription.'

Dad mumbles, 'What about school? You can't miss it. I'll collect them myself later.'

But he can't and there's no one else. Mum is in Berlin and Dad won't tell Uncle Kwame about this. I can't leave him alone.

'Isn't it your first day at the new job?' I ask, sitting beside him.

'I've called them.' Dad shifts slowly on the sofa bed.

I send a message from Dad's phone to my school saying that I'm too sick to come in today. I hope Mrs Morris forgets all about it by Monday.

'I'll be quick.' Forcing my trainers on my feet, I put on two hoodies, leave the flat and head towards town.

To Mum: ~~I don't know what to do~~

~~are you ever coming back~~

~~it's bad here~~

~~we need help~~

hi mum

She calls instantly; the background is noisy, so I can't hear her properly. 'What did you say, Mum?'

'Sorry, class is about to start. Give me a second,' she says. A door opens and closes, shutting out the noise in the background. *'Are you OK, Isaiah?'*

Mum always knows when there's something wrong, but she's in a different country now. It's not far, but it might as well be. Dad is right. It's just me and him now. 'It's nothing. I'm all right. I'm about to go to school now, so I'll call you later.'

'Are you sure? What's wrong?'

'Nothing. I'm *always* gonna be all right. I'll speak to you later, Mum.'

'OK, OK. I know when someone is trying to get me off the phone. Have a good day at school and I expect you to video-call me next time. I want to see your face. I miss it.'

A message pops up from Kieran.

Kieran: y aren't you in school?
I waited for you.

Me: headache

Kieran: is it arthritis?

Me: nah, it's gastritis

I laugh at the screen.

Kieran: it's definitely gloss-itis
I pass the corner shop on my
way to the chemist.

Me: it's corner-itis

Kieran: u made that word
up 😆

I feel bad for lying to Kieran because, out of all my friends, I tell him the most. But Dad doesn't like people knowing what's wrong with him. I think he thinks he'll be completely healed one day.

Kieran: you coming to mine after school?

Me: yeah

The pharmacy bell dings as I go inside. The pharmacist, Nikki, knows me well as we have an arrangement for me to collect Dad's medication.

I leave around ten minutes later with the white package tucked into my hoodie.

Much later, I push Kieran's door open; he's playing *FIFA* from his bed and Fredrick is on the floor.

Fredrick sticks out his leg, stopping me from moving closer. 'Kieran said you were sick. I don't wanna catch it from you.'

I dive on Fredrick, putting him in a chokehold as we pretend to wrestle. 'Tap out!'

Fredrick taps repeatedly on the floor. 'I'm tapping out!'

I grab a controller and Kieran begins a new game. 'Anything happen at school?'

'Not really,' he replies. 'Mrs Morris was looking for you.'

I stop. 'What did she want?'

'Same old, but I told her you were sick,' Kieran replies. 'Mr Iyer was asking about you too. I figured out what I'm gonna call my trainer business. "Kieran Kustomises".'

I start laughing and Fredrick joins in. 'What kinda name is that?'

He shrugs it off. 'At least I *have* an idea.'

All you can hear is the clicking noises from the controllers.

'Are you sure you can't come to the cinema tomorrow, Isaiah?' Fredrick asks, biting into a doughnut and licking the jam off his finger.

'Go and wash your hands!' Kieran shouts, grabbing the controller before Fredrick can touch it again.

Kieran's mum knocks, opening the door to the bedroom. '*Les garçons, le dîner est prêt.*'

'*On mange quoi, Maman?*' Kieran asks.

'I made Isaiah's favourite. Spaghetti and meatballs with garlic bread. Darius is joining us for dinner too.'

Darius is Kieran's older cousin who is into music. I see him singing on the street and at events.

Kieran tries to elbow me out the way to get to the table first, but I'm too quick for him, swerving under his arm.

My fork slams into the ceramic plate after taking a big bite of the spaghetti.

'Slow down, Isaiah. You'll choke on the food if you're not careful,' Kieran's mum says.

'That's how Isaiah always eats, Mum, like he doesn't

have food at home,' Kieran jokes, and the spaghetti clumps in my throat.

I stab at the pasta. 'I *do* have food at home.'

Kieran stops chewing and replies, 'I was joking, man. I know you're not poor.'

I laugh with my friends, but the spaghetti doesn't taste the same any more.

'What were you boys up to in there?' Kieran's mum asks.

'We were talking about our IT projects,' Kieran answers. 'Isaiah still doesn't know what he wants to do for his. If he doesn't choose soon, he'll get in trouble with Mr Iyer.'

I kick Kieran's leg under the table. *Why does he have to tell his mum everything?*

Fredrick's face twists in pain. 'Ow! Why did you kick me?' He tries to kick me back.

'Please behave, boys. And I don't want you to get in trouble, Isaiah,' she replies, concerned like my mum would be if she was here.

'I had Mr Iyer too.' Darius gulps down some water. 'Is this the one where you have to come up with your own business and create the website?'

'Yeah,' I reply.

'What are you good at?' he asks. 'You're always reading something.'

'I fix stuff. I'm helping my dad with jobs again.'

'Oooh, very practical,' Kieran's mum says.

'That's it.' Kieran's voice is muffled because his mouth is stuffed with spaghetti.

Kieran's mum leans towards him with a paper napkin. *'Avale avant de parler, Kieran. On se tient bien à table.'*

'Je suis désolé, Maman,' Kieran apologises, and swallows his food. 'I was trying to say that Isaiah should do a handyman business.'

'You know what, I'm gonna do that.' I grin.

'Mr Iyer's project helped me with setting up a real business,' Darius interjects. 'Outside of my job at the dog groomers, I teach kids how to play the piano using webinars, but I remembered everything we learnt in IT about setting up the website.'

Kieran's phone rings.

'Het is mijn vader.' He rushes to answer it as his dad's face pops up on the screen. *'Pap. We zijn aan het avondeten met Fredrick en Isaiah. Waar ben je nu?'*

Kieran's dad is a pilot, which means he works half of the month. He flies to places like Thailand, America, Canada and Dubai.

'Ik ben in een hotel in Ottawa.'

Fredrick stops eating and leans into the camera. 'I've been to Canada before with my family.'

'Ah, what did you see there?'

'I didn't know you've been to Canada,' Kieran says. 'Did you go to Niagara Falls?'

They all talk about Canada and other places they've been. When Mum and Dad were together, we didn't fly a lot, but we went on loads of trips around the UK and Ireland – sometimes in a caravan.

'I have to go now,' I say, feeling like the odd one out. 'Thanks for the spaghetti and meatballs, Mrs A.'

'Let me pack some for your dad, Isaiah,' she suggests, getting up from the table. 'I wouldn't want all this food to go to waste.'

Chapter Twelve

Monday

'Why is your phone holder so good?' Fredrick whines, studying his own project in our DT lesson. 'My one keeps giving me blisters and the pieces aren't fitting together.' He pesters me.

'Here.' I take a piece of sanding paper, throwing it in his direction. 'It's because you haven't sanded down your wood properly.'

'Show me how to do it, please.'

I take the block of wood, shaving the top and sides for him with another piece of sanding paper. 'It's easy, man.'

'Nice sanding, Isaiah,' Mrs Franklin says. 'You can start on your second project next lesson.'

Once the lesson is finished, us three are walking down the corridor, when Kieran catches my attention.

'Isaiah, look who's coming,' Kieran warns, pointing further down the crowded corridor.

It's too late to run. Mrs Morris spots me, calling me over.

'Hi, miss,' I say. 'How are you today?'

'Don't start with me this morning, Isaiah,' she replies, not taking the bait this time. 'You weren't in school on Friday. It's becoming a habit.'

'I was sick, miss, and you wouldn't have wanted me to come in and infect everyone . . . with everything happening around the world.'

Mrs Morris squints until her eyes are tiny slits. 'Why do you always seem to have an answer for everything, Isaiah?'

The bell rings for the next lesson, giving me a chance to get away. 'We can't be late for lesson, miss. You're always saying how important education is.'

She lets me go without saying anything else, which worries me because she never lets anything go.

'Class, we're going to be planning your websites today,' Mr Iyer explains. 'From now on, all our lessons will be focused on it.'

'I'm gonna do mine on video-game reviews,' Fredrick says. 'People buy the games and pay me to play and review it for them before they play.'

'If they've already bought the game, why wouldn't they just play it for themselves?' I ask, writing notes on my business.

Kieran chuckles. 'Isaiah is right.'

'I'm still perfecting it,' Fredrick says, shaking his mouse. 'And all of us can't be like you, Isaiah.'

'Of course not. I'm one of a kind. Even Mr Paterson knows it. I'm representing the school for that history exhibition. He told me yesterday.'

'If you go into the drive, you'll see a document called "website design sheet".' Mr Iyer writes on the board. 'When creating a website,' *sniff*, 'the information must be accurate and the website easy to use. Please use this lesson to fill out your website design sheet. You will need a homepage and at least three other pages. I'll approve the designs and then you can get creating the websites themselves. Here's an example of how you structure a website.'

Mr Iyer shows us a website on what weird pets you can own. Each pet had its own page and a description with a picture beside it.

Pygmy Goat, Micro Pig, Capybara, Tarantula, Octopus, Chinchilla, Madagascar Hissing Cockroach . . .

'Yuck!' Kirsty yells. 'Who would want a *cockroach* as a pet?'

'Yeah, man – that's disgusting,' Fredrick agrees, trying to get Kirsty to notice him.

When Dad and I were in one of those temporary houses before we got our flat, it was full of cockroaches and those things *weren't* pets.

'Hissing Cockroaches are very gentle actually,' Kesia

comments, and everyone turns to stare at her. 'The only thing is they do sort of hiss when you touch them at first.'

'How do you know that?' Kirsty asks.

'I have one,' Kesia adds. 'I collect insects.'

'She's weird,' Fredrick whispers. 'Don't you think Kirsty's hair looks nice today?'

I ignore him and focus on Mr Iyer.

'Your homework is to come up with your domain name.'

At lunch, we're in the playground watching some of the older boys playing basketball when Mr Paterson walks past the other side of the pitch. I chase after him.

'Sir! I've been looking for you.'

'Well, you've found me,' Mr Paterson answers. 'I hope you're here to talk about the exhibition.'

'Yeah, I wanna do it and I'm gonna win.'

'That's what I like to hear. I'm leaving it up to both of your interpretations of "connections with the past", but I'd expect the pair of you to have something to contribute to this together and individually.'

'Wait? What do you mean "both"? You said you only chose me, sir.'

What about the prize money? He's not going to make me share it, is he?

'You and Kesia will make a *wonderful* team. She has already been prepped. You can use my online subscriptions for access to archives you might need access to. I'll leave scheduling the meetings to you both. How does that sound?'

'Kesia? I thought it was just me, sir.'

Chapter Thirteen

'My credit can't be *that* bad,' Dad says as the door closes behind me. 'This loan is to ensure my son and I remain in our home, while we deal with landlord issues.'

'If you're experiencing housing issues, please get in contact with your council or Citizens Advice. I'm sorry, Mr Oni, with your credit score, we can't approve a loan—'

Dad disconnects the call, throwing his phone on the sofa beside him in anger. He doesn't notice me standing in the doorway.

I pick up the letters on the mat. One is from my school. I open it.

```
Dear Mr Oni,
    I'm writing to notify you of Isaiah's
poor punctuality and attendance record.
We would like to invite you in to discuss
with  our  Welfare  Officer,  Mrs  Morris,
```

about next steps and to put an action
plan together.

I don't read the rest but scrunch up the paper and stuff it into my pocket. 'Hi, Dad. How was work?'

'Oh, Isaiah. I didn't see you there.' Dad erases his strained face like words off my whiteboard. 'Rick, my new boss, is great. The job is nothing like before, but it's a job. I'm thinking of asking Rick for more hours.'

'You can't—'

'What did I tell you before about that word?' Dad snaps, his strained face returning. 'It'll be fine. I'm feeling much better today. Friday was a minor setback, but today is a good day.'

He said this about the extra jobs and then he couldn't move the day after.

'In fact, when I get paid this week, I want to take you and your friends to the arcade. We used to go all the time, but we haven't been in a while.'

Because we can't afford it any more so I stopped asking for it. 'We don't have to go to the arcade yet. Why don't we wait a bit? We can go another time.'

'No, we don't *need* to wait.' Shaking his head, Dad speaks with a tight tone. 'I'm taking you and your friends to the arcade – that's final. You'll all have fun.'

'All right, Dad.'

The chimes of the clock tower ring out. *Ding. Ding. Ding.*

Our flat becomes grainy and I'm standing in the workhouse kitchen. Steel pots and pans line the long table with the cooks, dressed in white uniforms, standing behind it.

Jacob.

The room changes back to normal. I can't win that competition unless I get the best research, and the best research is him. I rush into my bedroom to get my whiteboard.

'I'm going to the library for my history project. I'll be back soon.'

'Text me if you're going to be late!'

Jumping down the stairs, my Jordans slap against the cement as I collide with Uncle Kwame.

'Whoa, young blood,' he says, steadying me before I fall. 'Why are you in such a hurry?'

'I have to go and meet someone,' I reply.

'Is your dad up there?'

Where else would he be?

'Yeah, he's up there.' I glance at my phone.

'I won't keep you then. Go and meet your friend.'

Broken pieces of a wardrobe have been left beside the bins. I drag them into the basement with me, throwing the broken wood inside the fireplace, and wait for the weird flame to burn.

Jacob appears in the fireplace with the same broom and disgusted expression as he brushes dust off his shoulder.

'*Thank goodness, you're here to help,*' Jacob exclaims. '*I'm glad you kept to your word. My father always taught me to never make a promise you can't keep.*'

If I want to win the prize money, this is one promise I *have* to keep. 'I'm gonna find your dad for you.'

'*Swear it.*'

'Swear what?'

'*I've learnt the hard way that people lie.*' Jacob smacks the ground with his broom. '*My father would never leave without a word. I know something else is going on. Swear you'll help me find him.*'

'All right! I swear it. Happy?'

'*Ecstatic.*'

I open the whiteboard case. 'What's your dad's name?'

'*Emmanuel Olaitan Akintola.*'

I write down Jacob's dad's name. 'What else can you tell me to find him? Where was he going again?'

'*My father is an entrepreneur and a merchant. In January, he sailed back to Nigeria to acquire palm oil and to help some of those still enslaved. It's the last time I heard from him, but I know he's not gone. He can't be.*'

Emmanuel Olaitan Akintola
Merchant
Ship to Lagos months ago

'Who ya talking to, boy? You should be sweeping the ash. Are ya getting lazy?'

'No, Mr Moore, sir.' Jacob shrinks back, his hands wringing the broom. 'I'm not getting lazy. I swear it. I'll do better.'

Mr Moore grunts, then I hear footsteps pacing away.

'That's the workhouse guardian you were talking about in your letter.'

'He's a spiteful man! If he thinks we're getting lazy, he'll punish us. Mr Moore can lock you in a cell for the whole day without food or make you do hard labour or you might even receive . . . whippings. I wish I'd been taken to the Mayfair workhouse one town over. I heard that they even had a proper Christmas dinner.'

'You can't stay there. Isn't there anywhere else you can go until we find your dad? Anyone that you can stay with? A friend of your dad's? I have my uncle Kwame. He's my dad's friend, but he's like family.'

Jacob thinks for a second and sweeps the ash from the fireplace. 'I've got it! You're a clever one, Isaiah. I do have such a person. My father's associate, Raymond Parker, who's always been very fond of me. The only concern is that he lives in Manchester and I have no funds to get there.'

'Can't you figure out a way to make money? I need to find a way to make money too because . . . because . . . it doesn't matter, but you can't – we can't give up. My dad always says that we can do *anything*.'

'*Mr Moore does allow us to seek outside work, but it's not that simple,*' Jacob says, frustrated.

'What's something you're good at?' I ask, thinking about what Darius said to me.

'*I recently mastered Beethoven's "Moonlight Sonata", but I doubt I'll be able to get my hands on a piano here.*' Jacob tuts. '*You said you need the money. Why don't you get a job that you're good at then?*'

I ignore the way Jacob says it because he gives me the best idea. 'I can make my handyman business into a *real* one and fix things to make real money.'

'*Manual labour?*' Jacob's nose wrinkles. '*When my father came over to this country, he was an apprentice. He told me about all the hard work he had to do. Are you quite sure?*'

I stand up straighter. 'Yeah, I *like* fixing things. Why don't you ask some of the boys in the workhouse to help you find work?'

'*They won't be able to help me. I'm not like them,*' Jacob replies in a snobby way.

But they're like me. I bet that's what he's thinking.

Ding. Ding. Ding.

'Look, I've got to go now.'

'*Until next time, Isaiah.*'

Chapter Fourteen

Tuesday

'Isaiah, you're going to be late for school!' Dad calls. 'And Kieran said if you don't come out now, he won't give you the double sausage and egg bagel his mother made for you!'

I love Kieran's mum's breakfast bagels. She toasts the bagel so it crunches when you bite into it.

'Coming!' I shout back, tightening the loose bolts on my bed frame with a screwdriver.

At school, in between all our lessons, Fredrick kept on sneaking glances at what I was writing.

Isaiah's Grand Plans
- Finish IT site / start business
- Earn real money
- Get enough for late rent payment
- Help Jacob find his dad and get out of the workhouse / steal all the knowledge from Jacob's

head for the exhibition presentation
- Win the exhibition prize money too
- Get Mum to come back for the private exhibition
  so she can remember why she never should've left
  in the first place

I snort, turning away from him. 'Stop looking at my whiteboard.'

'Show me what you're writing then.'

'What's he got a case of, Kieran?' I say.

'Of nosy-itis!' Kieran teases. 'But I kinda wanna see what you've been writing too and where did you get the whiteboard from?'

'Now *you've* got nosy-itis.' I put the whiteboard in my bag. 'And it's nothing special. Just some notes and my dad got it for me.'

I pretend like I don't see them sneak a glance at each other.

In the corridor, the door to the school's sensory room opens. Kesia emerges, bumping into us.

'Are you following me again?' I ask bluntly.

Fredrick nudges Kieran and they laugh, but stop once Kesia joins in. 'Isaiah, not everything revolves around you. We're at school. Also, Mr Paterson said we need to meet for the history exhibition project.'

Why did Mr Paterson have to choose Kesia for me to work with? She thinks she knows everything.

I cough. 'Yeah, uh, we can talk about it during the next lesson.'

'OK, but we don't have a lot of time,' Kesia replies before walking down the corridor.

'Isaiah, I thought you said Mr Paterson chose you to do it by yourself!' Fredrick shouts. 'You're such a liar. I knew he didn't just ask you.'

'Whatever. He still chose *me*,' I say. 'You know what? You're not coming to the arcade this weekend then.'

We stop at the library doorway and Nancy waves at me. I scowl back.

'What?'

'My dad is taking us to the arcade this weekend, but I think I'll get someone else to go.'

'I was just messing about,' Fredrick says. 'Isaiah!'

I wouldn't really go to the arcade without him, but right now I'm too angry to tell him that.

I stomp into the library, sit down at a computer and get the National Archives up. I search Emmanuel Olaitan Akintola and only one research link comes up. A birth certificate.

Name: Emmanuel Olaitan Akintola
Birth date: 1790
Date of death: 1855

Jacob was *right*. His dad wasn't dead – at least not in 1838 – so what happened to him then? And why does he have a date of death, but Jacob doesn't? I remove Jacob's fountain pen from my pocket, inspecting it. *How does he write with this?*

I walk over to Nancy's desk.

'You seemed upset before,' she remarks, scanning a large book.

I flash Nancy a quick grin. 'How can I be upset when I'm in here?'

She gushes. 'The library is such a special place, isn't it?'

'Yeah, it is.' I hold up the fountain pen.

'Oooh, what a beauty that is. If I'm correct, it looks like a steel-point fountain pen. You'll need an inkwell to write with and I happen to have some ink! I'm an amateur calligrapher.' Nancy slides a pot of ink across the desk from her overflowing bag. 'Enjoy.'

'Thanks, Nancy.'

After school, I stop outside the food bank, hiding my face under the hoodie. I hate having to come here.

I hand over a small list of things we need to Reggie. He runs the place.

'We have *some* of this, but not all,' Reggie says. 'Donations are down this week. I'll get a bag packed for you.'

'Oh hiya, I remember you from last week. You have diabetes so nothing with too much salt, sweets or fizzy, right?' Kesia's voice comes from the other side of the food bank.

What's Kesia doing here? Why is she everywhere I am?

She's talking to a young white woman with brunette hair swept over her shoulder. 'Yes, thanks. Do you still give out extra support flyers? My mum needs to know about the household support fund.'

Kesia puts a flyer into the bag. 'It's all in there.'

'Thanks. It's just until my new job does all their checks.'

Nodding, Kesia finishes packing the bag. 'It's for emergencies like yours. The fund can help with food and petrol.'

The woman makes a noise. 'This is only temporary. It'll get better.'

This is only temporary. Dad used to say that about our situation, but temporary became permanent and now it feels like we're running on a hamster's wheel with no end in sight.

'Here you go,' Reggie says, handing me a full bag. 'Fresh food usually goes as soon as it lands, but I still have these.' Reggie produces four ripe yellow plantain from under the table. 'Do you want them?'

'I love plantain. Thank you.' I balance them on the top of the bag, trying to rush before Kesia sees me, but Reggie places a hand on my arm.

'A few times a week we get some young people like you together to play some games at the arcade. Some tokens are donated from people in the community.'

The same tightness builds in my chest as I shrug him off and turn to leave. 'No, I'm all right.' Someone might see me with them. I'm not like all the other kids who come here.

'Isaiah,' Kesia says from behind me. 'What are you doing here?'

I try to hide the full bag behind my back, but it twists awkwardly between my fingers and her eyes go down to it.

'More like what are *you* doing here,' I snap.

But it's too late, Kesia knows.

Chapter Fifteen

Dad is tucked under a thick duvet in the living room. The heating is off because he won't get paid until the end of the week. The hold music on his phone plays on repeat, with worry etched deep into his face.

'Are you ready for my legendary plantain and corned beef stew?' I joke, even though my insides feel rotten. I pump the plantain in the air. 'Reggie had them lying about.'

'Nice one.' Dad's voice is completely flat.

I slice the plantain and fry it in oil for about five minutes on each side before turning the heat off. Cooking was the one thing my mum taught me when I was younger. I blend a tin of tomatoes and an onion together, pouring the mixture into a small saucepan. I add the remaining seasoning that we have in the cupboard and put the heat on low.

Kesia better not tell anyone about seeing me at the food bank.

I kick aside some discarded pieces of wood to sit down beside Dad. 'What's all of this?'

Dad files the sides of a wooden frame to match the rest of the straight edges. He adds it to a neat pile of finished work on the coffee table. There are trays, more frames, kitchen products and serving trays. The only reason I'm good at DT is because Dad taught me all I know.

'There's a huge online market for wooden homewares. Apparently, it's "trendy",' he replies, smoothing out the edges.

'Hello, Mr Oni, are you still there?'

Dad snatches the phone up from the table. 'Yes, I'm here.'

'Unfortunately, there's been a growing backlog of disability assessments—'

'Yes, but my appointment has already been rescheduled twice,' Dad rants. 'Do you think I want to spend my whole day waiting for you to answer the phone? All I need to hear is that you have an appointment for me.'

'You're in luck, Mr Oni, we've had a recent cancellation and we can offer you a slot.'

'Thanks. When is it for?'

I rush to get Dad a pen so he can write on the back of an old letter.

'*The appointment is for this week Sunday. If it's too short notice we can—*'

'No, no. It's fine. I'll be there.'

'*Perfect. I have booked you in. Thank you for your patience, Mr Oni.*'

'Sure. Thank you.' Dad drops the phone and leans back on his support pillow. 'Some good news.'

My phone beeps and a message from Mum pops up. 'Yeah. I'm gonna do my homework.'

Dad yawns. 'OK, son.'

Going into my bedroom, I close the door behind me, laughing at the 'meanwhile in Berlin' picture Mum's sent of a woman fighting a giant bratwurst.

Mum: Can't wait for you to
come and visit

Me: I can't wait for you
to come back to 🏳

Mum: I miss you.

Me: miss you too. Shepten has the best
🐟 and 🍟

I take out a stack of A4 printer paper from my bag that Nancy gave me earlier. I told her I wanted to write letters to a new friend. (She doesn't know that he's from 1838 obviously.)

Nancy said that 'the art of letter writing has been lost with our generation'. I didn't know exactly what she meant, but it does feel weird writing a letter instead of messaging.

Taking out Jacob's fancy fountain pen, I begin the letter like he would, dipping the pen clumsily into the ink. When I write, I scratch the paper at first but try again.

Dear Jacob,

I found out that your dad is still alive in 1838, but I haven't found out anything else. I just wanted to tell you that you were right. Have you found some way to make money yet? I'm going to fix things for people, like furniture and all that stuff.

I'm using your fancy fountain pen to write this letter, but I keep scratching through the paper. Biros are much easier! I'll look for more information on your dad. Let me know what's happening at the workhouse.

Isaiah

Sneaking out of the flat, I creep into the basement and throw rubbish into the fireplace, watching the strange-coloured fire consume my folded letter. the strange-coloured fire, watching my folded letter burn.

Before heading home, I take a detour to the other doors in our block to see if I can get people interested in my handyman business. I knock on the first door I come to.

'Who is it?' someone says from the inside.

'I'm a handyman,' I reply, not having thought about what I was going to actually say.

'We didn't ask for a handyman,' the person replies before opening the door. She's wearing a black tunic. 'You look a bit young to be a handyman. You're about my James's age. Don't you go to his school? What are you doing knocking on people's doors?'

I rush down the landing, leaving all her questions behind to try someone else – that was just a tester. I knock on another door. A girl of around six answers the door followed by her annoyed dad.

'May, what have I told you about answering the door?' He breathes out and looks down at me. 'How can I help you?'

'Hi. I'm asking around to see if anyone needs a handyman. I can fix things. My dad taught me. It's for my school project.'

'Do you have a website I can look at?' he asks. 'Or anything I can look at?'

I groan internally because I haven't even made the website yet. 'It's still under construction—'

The man closes the door before I've finished talking, but the last door I knock on stays open. Mr Lim. He has on a blue polo shirt with his inky hair styled all fancy like in one of those hair commercials.

'Hi, my name is Isaiah and I'm asking around to see if anyone needs a handyman. I can fix things . . . it's for my school project. My website is not ready yet, but it will be soon. Promise.'

'You've knocked on the right door, Isaiah,' he says. 'Because I am the *king* of sales. Come back here on Thursday, but before that be sure to find someone you trust to knock on doors with you. Someone older.'

'Nutella!' a young girl screams from inside the house, making Mr Lim jump.

'I must go. My daughter is mean when it comes to negotiations.'

Chapter Sixteen

Wednesday

Mr Paterson begins today's lesson, but I'm only half listening. There's only one more week for me to make enough money for the rent.

Handyman business – who can go round to
people's houses with me?
~~Dad~~

I can't ask Dad because he can't know I'm doing this.

~~Uncle Kwame~~

Uncle Kwame will figure out why I'm doing this and then tell Dad.

~~Kieran and Fredrick~~

I need someone older. *Who do I know that's older and won't tell?*

I've got it.

'Kieran, can I have Darius's number?' I whisper, trying not to draw attention to myself.

'I'll send it,' he replies. 'One second.'

His fingers move under the table as he hides his phone. *Ping.* 'Why do you want my cousin's number?'

Fredrick's pretending not to listen, but half of his body is turned toward us and his pen stops moving across the page.

'I want to ask him about the website project,' I whisper back. 'He did it before, didn't he? I have some questions about it.'

Kieran squints, but I can't tell him more because he'll want to know.

'Mia, here's the magic pen,' Mr Paterson says, waving a normal black board pen around. 'Up you get, my scribe. Year Eights, we've looked at some of the positives of the Industrial Revolution, which were—'

'Steam trains,' I call out.

Mr Paterson rolls his eyes dramatically. 'You and these engines, Isaiah. What else?'

'Jobs,' Fredrick replies.

'Better wages.'

'More factories,' Kesia says. 'Production levels doubled too.'

'Oooh, a double whammy, Kesia. Anyone else?'

'It . . . uhh . . . improved other processes,' I answer. 'Like they could build better buildings and they could mass-produce stuff.'

'Another double whammy! Thanks for your answers, everyone. We're going to now look at the negative impact that the Industrial Revolution had. Let's backtrack for a second and consider the word "poorest" or "poverty". Fredrick, your turn to come and write. Class, tell Fredrick what comes to mind when you hear the word "poverty".'

'Ripped clothes.'

'Old trainers,' Kieran says to me, and I laugh a bit, but I'm not really into it. If Kieran knew that I had to draw on my trainers to hide the rips before I got my Jordans, what would he say? Would he still want to be my friend?

'Can't afford to buy food.'

'Nowhere to live.'

'Broke!'

Each time they say answers, it sounds like they are talking about Dad and me. My muscles quiver thinking about getting kicked out by our landlord and having nowhere to live.

All at once, the SMART Board at the front becomes

grainy, flickering black and white, transforming into part of an old-fashioned hospital. In the last metal-rung bed, there's a tall black man lying down with low-cut hair and bandages on his head.

The board changes back as Mr Paterson puts on a video. 'We're going to watch a short film on the kinds of jobs the lower class had back then. I want you to think . . . how did the Industrial Revolution negatively impact the poorest of society?'

The video flashes on, showing a cotton mill. There are really young children stood by the gigantic machines with sad expressions on their grimy faces. *Why are there children there?*

'On your sheets, write down a list of problems associated with these jobs and categorise them into their correct headings.'

'Imagine doing all that work and then the boss doesn't even wanna pay you,' Kieran says, flipping over his sheet.

'Oh gross!' Fredrick covers his mouth in surprise. 'Did you see that some of those kids could get their arms or legs chopped off in the machines?'

'Yeah, I saw,' I reply, feeling sick as I think about Jacob. 'Let's add that to the list.'

   – Child labour – kids made to work instead of
     going to school

- Workers had bad living conditions
- Long working hours - kids could collapse
- Factory workers were stressed and treated badly
- Malnourishment was a serious issue
- Dangerous machines

Mr Paterson gets our attention back to the board so we can share what we wrote down on our sheets.

'. . . Yes, thank you. The poor working and living conditions also caused diseases, but they didn't have the NHS then.'

'What! No NHS?' someone yells. 'But what did they do then?'

'If they had any money they could pay for a doctor, but most would make do with homemade remedies. As you can ghoulishly imagine, wounds were often left to rot and fester because there was nothing else that could be done. Many of the poor would ultimately succumb to infection or diseases.'

It's the same now, isn't it? They don't really care about Dad or his pain – maybe because they call it an invisible disability, that makes him invisible too.

'In fact, the Industrial Revolution also widened the gap between the rich and the poor because it was the rich people who owned the means of production, and the rest were workers. From the video, what were some of the views towards those who were poor? Yes, Kesia.'

'Some people believed that the poor only had themselves to blame and didn't want to help them,' Kesia answers.

'Correct. For your homework, I want you to write a letter to Queen Victoria explaining what life was like for someone in a factory. Thanks for sharing your brains with me today. Off you go.'

As the class files out, Mr Paterson tells Kesia and me to wait behind. 'How is my dream team getting on?'

Kesia slams a folder on the table with a sticker that reads 'History Exhibition' on it. *When did she have time to do all that?*

Great. Mr Paterson's going to think I haven't done anything, but I've been doing other important stuff, haven't I?

Moving in front of Kesia, I say, 'I already have an idea of what I'm doing for my part.'

Mr Paterson unwraps his turkey sandwich, taking a bite. 'Let's hear it.'

'Remember you asked about that Victorian newspaper clipping? Imagine if I could talk to someone from the past and have diary entries from them. Letters from the past. I thought I could make it like that.'

Like the ones Jacob writes to me.

'See, I knew I was making the right turkey – I mean decision.' Mr Paterson's stomach growls like a grizzly bear. 'Tell me more.'

'I'm going to write letters from a boy who lives in Cricklewood Workhouse and have my own response to him, so it's like a connection to the past. And . . . and a mystery!'

'Splendid. I can't wait to hear what else you both come up with together. We can check back next lesson.'

'Thank you, sir. I will share what I have then.' Kesia pulls the folder to her body, giving me a look before leaving the classroom.

'Can I use your library membership, sir? You know, for research.'

'Of course,' Mr Paterson says. 'Now, tell me more about this "mystery".'

'The boy from Cricklewood, his dad went missing, but I can't find out why.'

'You have to dig, Isaiah. There are loads of reasons why someone might go missing, but you must explore. Where were they spotted last in the past?'

Chapter Seventeen

'Laters, Isaiah,' Kieran says as I cross the road outside school, walking towards the flat.

Fredrick sniggers. 'Have fun with your new friend Kesia!'

I pretend I don't hear him and call Darius. The phone rings for a few seconds and I don't think he's going to answer, until he does.

The sound of water rushing in the background almost drowns out Darius's voice. *'Isaiah.'*

'How did you know it was me calling?'

'Kieran said you might. Hold on.' The water suddenly stops running and Darius says, *'Out you get, Basil.'*

'Basil? Who's that?'

'A very shy poodle dog.' Darius laughs. *'I'm at work. One day I'll make it big with music, but I'll be washing dogs until then.'*

'That's what I wanted to talk to you about. Remember that website business project you did? I'm doing a handyman business, but I need someone older, like you, to come to the houses with me when I fix things. You could promote your new EP.'

'Is that for Mr Iyer's IT class?'

'Yeah.'

Darius is silent for a moment. *'I don't remember us actually having to run the business – just creating the website . . .'*

Is he going to say no? If he doesn't say yes, who else can I ask?

'Yeah, I'll help you, but I don't have much time between shifts here. When do you want to start?'

I don't want to sound too desperate. 'Whenever you want.'

'OK. I'll need to check my rota.'

When I get off the phone, I run towards the basement to see if Jacob has left me a letter in reply to my one.

Lighting the fire, I watch the flame burn and a torn newspaper piece sits in the ashes.

Dear Isaiah,

I knew my father was still alive! I am forever in your debt. Do you know where he is?

It's getting worse every day here.

The job hunt is not going well. Excuse the poor penmanship. I had to use wooden sticks with steel needles and ink. And they have someone monitoring the ink! Can you believe it?

I'll let you hang on to my fountain pen for now, but I do want it back eventually. It was a gift from my father, and fountain pens are extremely difficult to get. You must throw one of your future pens through the fire for me to write with.

Yours truly,
Jacob

I scribble a quick letter back to Jacob.

Dear Jacob,

I'm starting my furniture fixing business tomorrow. I was researching what else you can do for work. What about chimney sweeping or shoe shining or being like a street entertainer? You have to try something else.

Isaiah

I throw a biro pen from my pocket and the letter into the fireplace and head towards the public library.

When I get outside, part of the street is grainy and

flickering. A coachman pulls the reins, calming down a black horse.

'Easy, boy!'

When I look again, everything is back to normal as if I'd imagined it. The clock tower is visible in the distance. I almost jump in surprise as Kesia appears beside me out of nowhere.

'Did I scare you?' she asks, her plaits blowing in the wind.

'You'll have to do better than that to scare me.'

Kesia shoots me a glance and infuriatingly starts walking in time with me. 'We'll see about that.'

I narrow my eyes at her as she tries to walk faster than me. She puffs and her legs pound the pavement as we run towards the library's entrance.

'I won!' she shouts.

'It's not a competition! And you didn't win; my foot was inside the library before yours.'

'Quiet in the library, please,' the librarian says, spying over the top of the bookshelves. 'I don't want to have to ask you both to leave.'

Kesia and I walk towards the computers. She makes it into another match of who can get there first and sign into the computer, drawing another disapproving look from the librarian.

Kesia plonks her folder filled with research down between us on the table. 'Let's get to work.'

My eyes grow. 'How do you do all of this with sickle—' *I didn't mean to say that out loud, but I've always wondered.*

'How do I do all of this with sickle cell?' Kesia takes the pages out one at a time without looking at me. 'I have good and bad days. I get pains sometimes in my joints. It's warmer now so it is usually better. The cold affects me more.'

'Like my dad,' I say, accidentally sharing something I haven't even told my friends. 'He has chronic pain from an accident at work. Dad can't do his job properly any more cos of the nerve damage in his back.'

'Is that why you were at the food bank? Because your dad is out of work? We used the food bank a—'

'Don't tell anyone you saw me there, all right,' I blow up and then I feel bad. *She can't tell anyone.* 'That was one of the only times. Who even needs that place? Let's just do this exhibition work so I can go.'

'You don't have to be rude, Isaiah,' she replies. 'I get it. I was saying that my family used the food banks before too, so I get it. I would never tell.'

Does she really?

'I'm sorry.'

'Apology kinda accepted.' Kesia flicks the plastic wallets in her folder hard so they slap into each other.

I half-smile.

'I've started doing research on the background of Shepten. I want to show people a map so they can see what it was before and what it is now.'

'That's actually a pretty good idea.'

'I've done a rough sketch on paper but I'll design most of it on the computer. And then we go on to your letters. I thought that, when we present, our personal speeches should come last,' Kesia explains. 'We can say what our connection is with the past and what we've learnt. Judges like it when you apply the project to yourself and make it personal. If you want, we can work on the letters together.'

'Why don't *I* look after the letters and you do the map.'

'Well, if you're sure, but *I* think we should do it all together because that's why Mr Paterson chose us.'

'Do you always listen to what people say?' I ask.

'No, but . . . fine!' Kesia throws her hands up in the air and the librarian glares at us. 'Have it your way, but we're still meeting and going over everything because the exhibition is only in a few weeks now so we're technically behind.'

'I can't meet every night,' I reply, because when am I going to do handyman jobs if I'm stuck in the library every evening?

'OK, I'll start putting the map together myself with short descriptions.'

'And I'll start working on the letters.'

After a while, I tilt my computer screen slightly so Kesia can't see what I'm doing. I need to find Jacob's dad. *What should I search for?* Mr Paterson said I need to dig for information. *What was the name of the ship he was on?*

Using Mr Paterson's password, I type in 'Emmanuel Olaitan Akintola' in the ship registry site, but nothing comes up because Jacob's dad didn't own the ship.

'You won't find anything that way,' Kesia says, typing on her keyboard. *How did she even see my screen?* 'You need to know the name of the ship to find the person on the ship.'

I move the screen again. 'All I have is their name.'

'What day did the ship set sail?' Kesia types on her keyboard.

'I don't need your help.' Shaking my mouse, I click on random things on the screen. 'And I don't have the day, only the month. January 1838.'

Kesia stops typing. 'Is this for our project?'

'Kinda.'

She resumes typing. 'OK. I think there were around five major ports in the UK at that time. Because you don't have the ship's name or a specific date, we have to go through *all* the passenger registers for that month.'

'How do you know all of this?' I ask, because it's usually

me that knows it all. 'Look how many pages there are. It's gonna take us ages to find him and the ship.'

'Do you want to find him or not?' she asks, pausing. 'If it's important to the project, we should find whoever it is you're looking for.'

After scrolling for some time my finger aches, but I finally spot his name. 'Look! Emmanuel Olaitan Akintola was on *Roman's Chance.*'

'Let me check the newspaper archive . . .' Kesia says. 'Oh! I think I've found something about that ship.'

'What?' I ask, leaning closer to her computer screen.

MORNING CHRONICLE
JANUARY 10, 1838

SHIPS LOST AT SEA
Avon
Roman's Chance

Chapter Eighteen

Thursday

'You all should have chosen a domain name for your website because we need to move on,' Mr Iyer says. *Sniff.*

Fredrick plays a game on a hidden tab so Mr Iyer can't see. 'I've decided that my new business is to make up business names for other people.'

'It's only cos you can't think of what else to do.' Kieran laughs.

'You're right,' Fredrick says. 'But at least I have something. I bet you don't have a name for yours yet, Isaiah.'

'Yeah, I do.'

I don't.

'What is it then?'

Somehow the whole class is listening, including Mr Iyer. 'It's . . . Matthew & Sons,' I reply, the name coming into my head. 'Matthew is my dad's name and I used to help him fix stuff when I was younger. My business is a handyman business. You see, I'm keeping it in the family.'

Mr Iyer ponders for a second. 'A family business. Smart. It'll be nice when you explain it as part of your assessment PowerPoint. Class, what Isaiah is doing is what you should be thinking about. Linking.'

Fredrick shakes his head. 'Why does everything always work out for you?'

'I dunno. Just how it is.' I grin, but it's ironic because loads of things don't work for me. My friends don't know that.

'Today we'll be focusing on researching for your website.' *Sniff.* 'By the end of the lesson, you'll understand what sort of information you need . . .' Mr Iyer goes on, but I've stopped listening.

'Did you speak to Darius?' Kieran asks, and I nod. 'What did you talk about?'

I knew he was going to ask.

'I'm making my handyman business into a real one so I can get extra money . . . other than the money I get from my dad, you know. Darius is coming with me to people's houses as a kind of chaperone. It was all my idea.'

'Swear? That's sick. Why didn't I think of that?' Fredrick says to himself.

'Won't that be a lot to do, with school as well?' Kieran asks, lowering his voice so only I can hear.

'I can do everything. It'll be easy.'

'When are we going to the arcade with your dad again?' Fredrick asks. 'I've got tokens to use.'

Dad's been working longer hours this week to earn extra money. I suddenly feel guilty that we're just gonna spend it on arcade games.

'Umm . . . On Saturday, but don't forget to bring those tokens with you. I can't wait to play Kart Racing Extreme.'

Kesia leans over the top of my computer. 'Did you do any more research on Emmanuel Akintola?'

'Not yet.'

Kesia's eyes gleam like the strange fire in the basement. 'In the eighteen hundreds, one in seven ships that left ports on a voyage either disappeared or were known to be lost at sea.'

But I know Jacob's dad isn't lost at sea. I just don't know where he is.

Once Kesia moves back to her seat, Fredrick can't resist it. 'She's your new bestie.'

'Boys, are you listening back there?' Mr Iyer asks. 'You should be getting on with the website research.'

'Yes, sir,' I respond.

We're walking home when a voice note comes up from Mum. I play it.

'Hi, Isaiah.' She yawns into the phone. *'Sorry, I wanted to*

114

check in with you. How's your history project going? How are things with you and your father? I'm still working out when I can come to see you, but it doesn't look promising. They've set us this important assignment and my job is low on staff right now. I will keep you updated. Love you.'

She *promised*. She's let me down. Again.

'I know how it is with my dad being gone for weeks sometimes,' Kieran says, shoving his hands into his pockets. 'It's rubbish – even with all the things he buys me. It's not the same.'

It's not the same because Kieran will never have to worry about food or heating or getting kicked out of his house. It's not the same because Kieran's family is still together.

'I'll chat to you later,' Kieran says. 'Can't wait to go to the arcade.'

'Yeah, talk to you later.'

To Mum: ~~You promised~~

When I get into the flat, it's unexpectedly full of laughter as Uncle Kwame is in the living room with Dad.

'Young blood, you're here,' Uncle Kwame says. 'Your dad and me are talking about the good old days. We used to be part of this group of friends and we did *everything* together.'

Dad has his body propped up at the corner of the sofa. 'When the Isley Brothers toured in the UK, we camped outside so we could be right at the front. It happened to be the rainiest weekend of the year.'

'I had mud where I thought mud couldn't reach!' Uncle Kwame bellows. 'Oh man, we used to do the craziest things together. We were tight.'

I guess Dad's changed. I know he hasn't told Uncle Kwame about the landlord trying to kick us out because he'd do anything to help.

'I heard you're following in your father's shoes,' Uncle Kwame says, 'with this business of yours.'

My back straightens. 'What do you mean?'

Dad wipes his brow, looking at me funny. 'For your IT project, son, you're doing a handyman business, isn't it? You have to make a website for it. You can't have forgotten already.'

'Oh, yeah.' I grin. The queasy feeling in my stomach dies down. 'My IT project. I'm calling it Matthew & Sons.' I throw myself on the sofa in between Dad and Uncle Kwame.

Smiling, Dad moves forwards to ruffle my hair, but I move out of the way. 'My son.'

Uncle Kwame slaps hands with me, making Dad smile harder. 'And that's what I like to see. Keeping it in the family. I know you're killing it at school with that brain of yours.'

'Yes, he gets that from me,' Dad responds.

And Mum says I get it from her.

I check my watch. 'Mr Lim downstairs is helping me with my project. I'm going over there to have my first lesson with him.'

'Mr Lim! He sold me all the new clippers for the barbershop. Before I knew it, I was buying bibs and all these extra items too.'

'Mr Lim from the bottom floor?' Dad asks, massaging a spot on his back. 'You know I *did* run a successful business for years, Isaiah. My knowledge and expertise is surely good enough for your project.'

'Matthew, relax,' Uncle Kwame says. 'Isaiah wasn't saying that your knowledge wasn't good enough. Isaiah is a smart boy. I know he has a reason why he didn't ask for your help.'

Swallowing to slicken my dry throat, I say, 'Of course you're the best, Dad. Mr Lim is just helping me with the website – that's all.'

When I get to Mr Lim's, he greets me with a handshake and teh tarik, which is a type of Malaysian tea. There was more condensed milk and sugar in it than tea, but I prefer it this way. Mr Lim's flat is similar to ours with the narrow corridor branching off into smaller rooms, but his flat is full of plants. I feel like I'm in a jungle.

'Thanks, Mr Lim.' I put the empty glass back on to the tiny saucer.

'Your first door-to-door sales tip is knowing your product,' Mr Lim explains, tapping on his framed 'salesman of the year' certificates from Kuala Lumpur and London. 'If you don't know your product, then you can't call yourself a salesman.'

I write it down on my whiteboard.

Know your product.

'Cut cut,' Mr Lim's daughter says with a knife and fork in her hand. She's staring at a small bowl with sausages in it.

He cuts it up for her. 'Another tip is to make a genuine connection.'

'That's easy,' I reply with my chin raised. 'I'm good with people. You've just got to tell them what they need to hear.'

'No,' Mr Lim insists. 'It's more than that, Isaiah. It's about *understanding* people. People appreciate talking about things they care about. You must connect with them, so they can call you back. If the customer has a dog, I make sure to ask about that dog or bring small treats for it next time. It's *more* than the money.'

Money and connection.

'They will use you again and again if you build a *trusting* relationship with them. How do you think my wife accepted my proposal?'

'You bribed her with your pulut kuning,' Mr Lim's son, who has large headphones on, says without looking up.

Mr Lim wiggles his eyebrows. 'Food is the way to a woman's heart. I understood the product.'

'I'm telling Ma you called her a product,' his son replies.

'Shouldn't you be doing your homework?' Mr Lim asks. 'That's another point. You need to be an expert at listening. I know my son isn't doing his homework because he's being a busybody. Actively listen so you can pivot. We should roleplay to check you've retained the gold I've given you. Isaiah, you be you and I'll be a customer who is tough.'

Concentrating, Mr Lim stands with his fingers tucked under his chin.

'Hi, do you need anything fixed in your house?' I ask.

'Who are you? I don't know you,' Mr Lim squeaks in a random high note, making me crack up. 'This is no laughing matter. You could lose your customer. Focus.'

'All right. Yes, you don't know me. My name is Isaiah and I live in the area. I have set up a handyman business for my IT project at school.'

'Get to the point,' Mr Lim says. 'People are busy. Jump right into why you're there.'

'I can fix TVs and furniture. Anything you need.'

'But I don't need anything! My old TV is perfectly fine.'

'Does it sometimes cut out or lose signal? I can help with that. I'll even polish the TV for you. You'll get a *full* service.'

'Good, good. It's easy for you to turn on the charm. You're ready for your first customer. The next time you come, I'll have something for you to fix as a test.'

Chapter Nineteen

Friday

'For my birthday, my mum is thinking of renting out this paintball place and getting food afterwards,' Kieran announces during Mr Paterson's lesson. 'If I do well at school, my parents said they'd make my birthday even bigger.'

'Bigger like what?' Fredrick asks. 'Are they flying you out somewhere?'

'Yeah, something like that,' Kieran boasts. 'My dad gets discounted flights so we're maybe doing a mini tour as a family.'

'That's dope. Where are you going?'

I haven't seen Mum in months now. I wish I could fly to see her.

'This is a poster for the Poor Law Amendment Act of 1834,' Mr Paterson explains. 'I'm not sure if I've already told you about the Poor Law. Have I? Say hocus pocus if I have.'

'What are you talking about, sir?' someone asks.

'None of you are fun. The Poor Law Act ensured that the poor were housed in workhouses, clothed and fed. This poster shows the poor relief on offer in the workhouse, which wasn't great. Can anyone guess what the conditions were like in workhouses?'

'Bad,' I reply, repeating what Jacob told me. 'They have to be up before five a.m. every day and they're given work to do like oakum picking.'

'Tell us more, Isaiah. What is oakum picking?'

I pretend I have rope in my hand. 'Yeah, so they're given old rope and they had to untwist it into many strands and then take those strands and unroll them. It makes tiny cuts in their hands, which sting. If they don't do their work right, they can be locked in rooms without food.'

'Workhouses sound like prison,' Fredrick remarks, his gloomy expression matching other people's around the room.

No one ever wants to be there but Jacob is.

'I think we can all gather that conditions in the workhouse weren't ideal.' Mr Paterson leans on his desk with his feet crossed in front of him. 'They were full of manual labour, cramped conditions and poor-quality food – no one would actively choose to live there. Now, we're going to look at Charles Booth. Does anyone know what he's mostly known for?'

Kesia raises her hand. 'The poverty map.'

Is that where she got the map idea from? I bet she read ahead.

'Correct,' Mr Paterson says. 'He organised one of the most complete surveys of London and he found that there were actually *more* poor people in London than everyone thought. It planted the roots for things that are relevant today such as the old-age pension. I want to throw the question out to the class: "Can we compare the poverty of then to now?"'

Kirsty's hand shoots up in the air. 'Poverty then was *way* worse than it is now. Weren't people dying in the streets of diseases?'

'Hmmm, interesting point,' Mr Paterson muses. 'Any other thoughts?'

'And we have cheap supermarkets and other places like that. Most people I know have houses now.'

'We're going to compare our views on poverty now with Booth's.' Mr Paterson switches the slide and Booth's map of London appears. 'We'll be looking at the similarities and differences, questioning the indicators of poverty today. For homework, I want you to write a diary entry from a child in a workhouse.'

As the class file out, Mr Paterson asks, 'How is everything

going? Did you find out anything else about your mystery missing man?'

'Yes,' Kesia interrupts before I can respond. 'We found out that the ship he was on went missing at sea.'

Why is she talking about it like she knows everything? She doesn't. She doesn't know Jacob. I do.

'Fascinating.'

'I read ahead and Charles Booth's map gave me an idea for our exhibition project,' Kesia rambles on, stealing Mr Paterson's attention.

I knew it.

'We're creating our *own* map of Shepten and comparing some of the places in the past to what they are now. Our block of flats used to be Cricklewood Workhouse, the school was a Victorian hospital and the food bank was a chapel.'

I knew all of that except the last one. *Why is she mentioning the food bank? And why is she showing off?*

'I knew I put my two *best* people on it!' Mr Paterson exclaims. 'I want to see something actually written down, so take the geniuses in both of your heads and put it on paper.'

'Thanks, sir.' Kesia scribbles in her notebook. 'We'll have a proper plan by next week.'

Mr Paterson moves back to the front of the class as the message that I've been waiting for comes through.

Darius: My shift got cancelled last minute.
Meet today? And I have some time off next week too

'Are you free after school? We can meet at the library,'
Kesia says. 'Or what about at the weekend?' She scribbles
down her number and slides me the slip of paper. 'We
need to start working on it properly because the exhibition—'

'I can't. I'm busy.'

She doesn't need me anyways.

'Why not? I thought you wanted to win. If you do, we
need to meet.'

'Course I wanna win,' I lash out. 'You do your part of
the project and I'll do mine. I've got stuff to do, not that
I have to explain myself to you.'

Chapter Twenty

Before I go to meet Darius, I rush down into the basement, pulling open the door as I normally do. The handle is surprisingly hot.

'Ow!' I yell, shaking my hand about.

I kick the rest of the door open with my foot. *When did the door get so hot?* I follow my usual routine of lighting the fire and watching the flame burn, waiting for Jacob to appear.

He does, but somehow he looks worse. He leans on his broom for support as he rubs at the bags under his eyes. Yawning, his sunken face moves in the flames.

'What happened to you?' I ask.

'It's this place, Isaiah. I haven't found a job and I dread the moments I spend sharing with all these boys. There is a layer of dirt on my skin that I can't scrub off, no matter how hard I try. The only piece of news that could possibly make this miserable day brighter is word on my father. Have you located him yet?'

'Yeah and . . . no.'

Jacob's eyes blaze through the fire. *'Well, which one is it? Where is my father?'*

'We . . . I found out the ship he was travelling on was called *Roman's Chance*, but . . .'

'But what? Out with it, Isaiah.'

'*Roman's Chance* is missing.'

At the word 'missing', the broom slips out of Jacob's hands, bouncing on the floor. *'Lost!'*

'There *has* to be something else out there about *Roman's Chance* . . . I promised I'd find your dad so that's what I'm gonna do.'

'He's lost at sea, Isaiah. What can you do from where you are?'

My heart beats in my throat. I swallow.

'I—'

Jacob is gone.

Chapter Twenty-One

Appearing from behind the bins, I walk up to Darius, tapping his shoulder.

'Where did you come from?' Darius asks, spudding me with his closed fist.

'The b— Meeting my friend.'

Darius looks around, trying to make sense of what I said. 'But—'

'I have the tools,' I interrupt, tapping on Uncle Kwame's toolbox, which I stashed earlier in the basement. 'We should knock on doors around the main road to start with.'

Darius points instead at my block. 'We should try your neighbours first and focus on one area rather than lots of different places.'

I shake my head. 'Why don't you wanna go somewhere else?'

'I'm sure you already know one or two people in the building and we can branch out after we've finished here.

Maybe someone who's moved in recently and needs help with their stuff?'

'You're right.' I remember what Mr Lim said to me about selling. 'Mr Lim said I should start on familiar territory.'

Darius makes a funny face. 'Does Mr Lim have black hair in a quiff and say "good" a lot?'

I burst out laughing because that's the best description of Mr Lim. 'Yeah, that's him.'

'He sold me a new washer dryer and he was only over to fix my internet connection.'

Mr Lim does it all! He did say to me, *It's important to wear many coats so you're able to change coats for the right price*. I think I get that now.

'I do know someone who just moved in. She might need some furniture fixed and some music to listen to.'

I knock on the door of the flat above us. Clarice opens the door; paint is splattered all over her orange overalls. 'Isaiah, to what do I owe this pleasure?'

Something warm and furry brushes against my leg. Garrett Morgan's rabbit nose twitches and Clarice picks him up.

'G.M., say hi to Isaiah and . . . Darius, is it?'

I look between the two of them. 'Do you know Darius?'

Darius taps his nametag from the groomers. 'I forgot I still have this on.'

Right, I need to focus on making money. 'Hi, Clarice, I have a handyman business for my IT project. It's called Matthew & Sons, which is named after my dad, who taught me everything I know.'

Clarice holds G.M. in front of her face, using a gruff voice with an American accent to speak for him. *'Isn't that precious?'*

'Do you have anything I can fix?' I ask. 'I can do it *all*.'

'As long as you know your way around Ikea furniture, you can come on in. When it comes to fixing things, our landlord is not a particularly helpful man.' I almost trip over a box in the centre of the room, which props up a large painting. 'Sorry for the mess. The gallery needs my new collection asap.'

'It's amazing to see another black artist killing it,' Darius comments. 'Do you have socials? I'd love to follow and maybe buy a painting.'

'That's very kind of you, but I'm not online much. You *can* find my work all over Shepten Gallery's socials though.' Clarice focuses her attention on me. 'I have a shelf and a chest of drawers with your name on it. You'd think since I work with my hands for a living, I'd be better at fixing things, but, no, when I sat on the chair I mended, I ended up with milk all over me!'

I hold in the laugh, picturing it.

'G.M., Isaiah thinks I can't see him trying not to laugh at me.' G.M. is busy chewing hay in the corner. 'How much are you charging?'

'Forty pounds?' Mr Lim said I should think about pricing so I try to go with what Dad charges. The landlord's deadline is coming up next Wednesday; I need any money I can get.

'Sold!' Clarice yells. 'Why don't you plug your music into the speaker, Darius? We can listen as we work. I need to get this new piece finished.'

Darius's first song comes through the speakers; he sings along.

Clarice nods her head and makes small brushstrokes. 'You need to send me the details of your next gig so I can come and support you.' She puts down the brush. 'Isaiah, I'll show you to the room.'

After a few hours and a text to Dad that I'm working late on my IT project, I'm done with the furniture.

'Look at it, G.M.!' Clarice exclaims. 'This is what correctly put together furniture is supposed to look like.'

'Can I take some pictures for my website?' I ask.

'Yes, yes. Take as many pictures as you like,' Clarice replies. 'I'm getting some more furniture in soon so I'll make sure to call you.' Clarice hands over a miniature painting of our building and the money for fixing. 'I was warming up my brushes the other day and I drew this. Shepten has such a rich history.'

'Thanks, Clarice.'

Chapter Twenty-Two

Saturday

Kieran: I can't wait for the arcade

Fredrick: what time are we meeting

Me: 2, I reckon. Let me
check with Dad

First, I have to find something for Jacob because I can't leave him thinking his dad is lost forever. Clarice said I could use her Wi-Fi since ours has been cut. I never told her why, just that our Wi-Fi is funny sometimes and she believed me. If Kesia was here, we would've found something by now, but I can do this myself.

If Jacob's dad didn't die, then where is he? The ship's register! I can see who the other passengers were and what happened to them. I pull up the register and search names in the archives.

Ezra Carter – presumed dead (lost at sea)
Arthur Johnson – presumed dead (lost at sea)
Violet James – presumed dead (lost at sea)

I trawl through pages of the newspaper archives on my phone, searching for anything on *Roman's Chance* . . . wait!

MORNING HERALD
JANUARY 25, 1838

Roman's Chance goes down in the English Channel, 50 presumed dead, many survivors rescued.

That's it! Emmanuel Akintola was a survivor!

Dad knocks before opening the door and leaning on the doorframe. 'Where did you get this fine painting from?' I forgot I'd left it on the kitchen table. 'It looks like a Clarice painting.'

'How do you know Clarice?'

Dad smiles warmly. 'I saw her walking her rabbit G.M. out front the other day.'

The smile is the same one Fredrick has when Kirsty talks.

Dad fidgets. 'Why did she give you a painting?'

My phone vibrates with a message from Uncle Kwame. *Phew.*

> **Uncle Kwame:** young blood, I thought you were coming to fix the chairs at the shop.

I throw the covers off me.

'Where are you going?'

'Uncle Kwame is helping me with my project.'

'We have the arcade at two.'

'I'll be quick, promise . . . and about the arcade, we don't have to go, Dad,' I say. 'I can tell my friends I'm feeling sick or something.'

'No.' Dad bristles. 'Of course we're going! I promised you we'd do this. I'm not gonna let you down.'

'What's good, young blood?' Uncle Kwame is shaping up a client's hair in the swinging black chair.

Music plays and he does a one-two step with the razor bobbing between his hands.

'Kwame, watch what you're doing with the razor!' the client in the chair cries. 'The last thing I want is a bad shape up.'

'Unc, where are the chairs you need me to fix?'

'What are you using the money for? Are you saving up for new clothes?'

'Yeah, and some other things.'

The barbershop bell *dings* and there's a strange smell of cigars. When I look around, it's the same barbershop it's always been.

'Come and let me show you where the chairs are,' Uncle Kwame says, leading me to the far corner of the shop.

I bend down by the large boxes, removing the instructions, when Uncle Kwame clears his throat behind me.

'I don't know if it's my place to say,' he murmurs, his voice almost as quiet as the tiny hairs landing on the barbershop floor. 'I've been noticing some things for a while now, but I haven't said because I thought it would resolve itself.'

I focus on reading the instructions, ignoring the feeling in my stomach like a bike doing wheelies. 'What would resolve itself?'

'I've been noticing your dad is getting worse.' Dad was never better. His pain is *always* worse. 'And I noticed that your flat . . . your dad blamed it on faulty wiring, but I know a place with no power when I see one. You're only thirteen, young blood. You shouldn't be fixing furniture for clothes.'

'It's not for clothes!'

The barbershop quietens.

'Then what is it for?' he says. 'Speak to me, Isaiah. If you need help, you must let me know.'

'It's nothing, Uncle Kwame,' I reply, not trusting myself to look him in the face.

'You can tell me anything. Even if you're feeling a little sad about your parents' divorce being finalised. It's normal.'

I stop screwing in the nails. 'It has?' *Why didn't anyone tell me?*

'I thought your dad told you.'

As I'm screwing in the nails, I don't realise how hard I'm pressing until the wood begins to splinter and sink beneath my fingernails.

'Young blood, watch your hands.' Uncle Kwame steps towards me, gripping my shoulders, but I shrug him off and rush through the barbershop.

'Isaiah!'

The late rent payments and now this. *What else is Dad not telling me?* I thought it was just us two.

A burst of anger shoots through me like a bullet. As I pass the tall mirrors, they suddenly darken, turning grainy and reflecting a Victorian store. *Uncle Kwame's barbershop in the past.* A woman in a pink silk dress and a fancy hat brings several jars to the counter. Flustered, the shopkeeper wipes at his round glasses as he tries to pack the groceries quickly.

In the corner, a young boy with a broom sleeps in a chair; his apron has the name 'William Webster' on it.

Albert. Albert! That's the second time you've fallen asleep today. You may be my nephew, but I can still dismiss you.

The mirrors go back to normal. I leave the barbershop and call Dad, but he doesn't answer. Mum does though.

'Why does no one tell me anything?'

'Hello to you too, Isaiah. What's happened?'

She's in Berlin living a different life.

A different life without me

'Nothing, Mum. I'll speak to you later.'

Chapter Twenty-Three

In the basement, I'm standing in front of the strange flame. I have two missed calls from Dad. Uncle Kwame must've called him.

> Dear Jacob,
>
> I wanted to check that everything was OK because you kind of just disappeared yesterday. I know you're upset but I promise we'll find your dad, so you can be together. He didn't go down with the ship, he survived! So that means he's out there, somewhere . . . It's not exactly the same, but I know what it feels like being kept apart from a parent.
>
> Anyway, I think I have a solution to your job problem. When I was at my uncle Kwame's barbershop, I looked through the mirror and saw a shop from your times. I think it's called

William Webster – maybe they will give you a job? The shopkeeper looked stressed today. His nephew was sleeping on the job! He might need more help.

Stay safe.

Isaiah

I throw the letter into the fireplace and head to the flat.

Dad sits up on the sofa once he sees me come through the door.

'Why didn't you answer your phone?' he asks, rubbing his head as if he's unjumbling his thoughts. 'Uncle Kwame called me.'

I don't say anything.

'I'm sorry. You shouldn't have found out like that.' The duvet hangs over his hunched shoulders. 'With everything going on . . . Are you not OK with it? You knew we were going to get divorced. We spoke about it.'

'Were you even gonna tell me?' I ask. 'You only told me about the rent problem because the landlord came here.'

'Is there anything else I don't know? Of course I would've told you,' he says, the duvet falling to the floor.

'What happens to me in the divorce?' I say, quietly.

'You know everything, son. The plans are the same. I'll

get sole custody of you while your mother is away studying, but we're revisiting that once she's back. Nothing will change.'

Why does it feel like everything already has?

Dad tugs at one of my cornrows. 'We have the arcade later. Why don't you get ready for that?'

I forgot about the arcade trip. *Do I even want to go any more?*

'Hi, boys,' Dad says as we make our way towards town. 'Are you both excited for the arcade?'

'Yeah!' Fredrick and Kieran shout together, making me feel better because for once it's *my* dad buying us something. I'm just hoping he can afford it.

'Isaiah, I know you're getting bare money now so you can buy us more tokens when mine run out,' Fredrick says.

I nudge Fredrick, mouthing, *What are you doing?* He'll ruin everything.

Dad scratches the sweat on his forehead and chuckles a little. 'Oh, and how is Isaiah getting all of this money?'

'He was joking,' I add quickly. 'When I'm older, I'm gonna make loads of money.'

Dad grabs me into a side hug as my heart races. 'Yes, my smart son.' Dad's phone rings. 'It's my boss, Rick. I have to take this call.' While Dad takes the call, my friends bring up my business again. *Didn't they get it before?*

'Why don't you want your dad to know you started a proper business?' Fredrick asks, confused.

'He won't be happy.' *Because he thinks he can look after everything, but he can't so I need to help.* 'You know how it is.' I grin. 'He'd prefer to give me money, so I focus on school.'

Dad gets off the call and immediately I know that something's wrong. 'Dad, is it about mon—'

He cuts me off with a nervous laugh. 'Don't worry about it. Let's go and have a good time.'

I thought he wasn't going to hide things any more.

As the anger builds inside me like a growing furnace, the muscles in my neck twitch.

The side street turns grainy, flickering black and white. There are a group of kids performing tricks for a small crowd. One kid is on his back and the other balances on his feet with his hands, but that's not what catches my eye. Two kids are kicking another, who shields his head on the floor. I know that head.

'Jacob?' I shout out but it's like he can't hear me.

He has a grazed knee and a split lip.

'Son, what is it?'

I move forward, but in another second the street is back

to normal as if I didn't see anything. 'Nothing . . . it's nothing.'

When we get to the arcade my heart sinks. Reggie from the food bank is here with a few other adults. Kesia and some other kids I recognise are eating pizza at the table.

Dad points towards the café counter. 'Two double meat feasts, a Sprite, a Coke and a Fanta coming right up.'

I glance up at Dad when he reels off all this, but he just nods and starts limping away before I can say anything.

Reggie sees me and waves me over.

'Who's that man waving?' Kieran asks, always noticing things that I wish he wouldn't. 'Do you know him?'

'I see him sometimes around Shepten.' I half lie. 'You lot can go on Kart Racing Extreme and I'll meet you there. Dad always forgets to order garlic bread.'

'Nothing can beat Fucchinis though,' Kieran comments.

'Nothing,' I repeat back.

I walk towards the counter but once I've seen Kieran and Fredrick have their backs turned, I take a detour to where Reggie and Kesia are.

'Glad to see you here, Isaiah,' Reggie says. 'Why don't you grab a slice? Tokens are in the pot for free games.'

I glance over to the car games then duck down and slide in the booth beside another boy sat opposite Kesia and another girl I've seen around. I'll be less noticeable if I'm sat down.

Kesia doesn't respond to me, instead narrowing her eyes.

'Hi, I'm Rowan,' the boy says, tightening the strap on his hat. 'We're playing Asteroids next. Want to come with us?'

I shake my head. 'I'm here with my friends.'

The rest of the group moves out of the booth, but I stop Kesia before she leaves. I can't resist letting her know that I know something she doesn't.

'Guess what, I found something interesting about *Roman's Chance*. There were *confirmed* survivors after the wreck. Jacob's dad must've been one of them.'

'That's nice,' Kesia says, but it doesn't *sound* nice. 'You can continue researching by yourself then. I'm going to ask Mr Paterson if we can do our exhibition presentations separately.'

'What? Why?' I breathe. 'Is it because of what I said before?'

'Because you only ever want to do things if it's done your way,' she replies. 'And that's not teamwork. If you need help, Isaiah, just say. You're so confident that you will win, so you can do it by yourself.'

Chapter Twenty-Four

Sunday

'You're not going to say anything?' Dad questions as we walk, slowly, to the assessment centre.

'Anything.'

'Very funny, smarty pants,' Dad says, roughing up my braids. I push him off softly.

'Watch my hair, Dad.'

'It's getting messy,' he comments. 'We need to take a trip down to your uncle's.' Dad angles his body away, resting on his cane so he can see my face properly. 'I'm sorry if it seems like I'm keeping things from you all the time.' The wind whistles, rustling the trees as we walk in silence. 'I didn't want to burden you with anything else. I'm grateful for you, son. I don't think you know how much.'

I want to tell Dad how hard everything has been, but I can't.

BZZT.

Darius: I have some free time next week. There are other people in the building who need things fixed.
Are you free after school?

Me: yeah

Darius: Tuesday then

The assessment building reminds me of our block. It's plain and made of weird-coloured brick.

'Hi, can I help you?' the person at the counter says. 'Do you have your appointment letter?'

'Yes, I have it here.' Dad pats his right trouser pocket for the piece of paper.

I slip the letter out of my jacket, handing it to him. 'Here it is.'

'Thanks. What would I do without him, eh?' Dad remarks, the skin around his eyes creasing as he squints. 'I have my two forms of ID here too or I'll be tossed out and have to wait another five years for an appointment.'

The receptionist ignores his comment, taking the documents and signing him in. 'The main lift is out of order, so you'll need to use the one around the side of the building to get to the third floor.'

Dad's tone is sour. 'Of course, silly of me to think it

would be working in an assessment centre for disabilities.'

'We sent a text to everyone who had an appointment today. It will be fixed by the end of the day,' she explains, but Dad ignores her, heading for the door. 'Unfortunately, children aren't allowed inside. We sent that information too. Your son will have to wait here for you.'

'It's all right, Dad,' I rush to say as his jaw ticks, ready to explode. 'I don't mind waiting. I brought my phone with me. They have free Wi-Fi.'

Dad grasps my shoulder. 'Hopefully I won't be gone for too long.'

I watch Dad leave and sit down to wait for him, making a list

Money total £40 from Clarice
Research more on Roman's Chance
Work on exhibition project ~~with Kesia~~

'You're so confident that you will win, so you can do it by yourself.'
Gazing out of the door, I wonder when Dad will be back and how long the assessment will take. I'm alone in the waiting room.

Why does Kesia think I want to do it by myself? Because I do . . . I did.

The chair creaks as I lean forward in it, drawing the

receptionist's attention. Why is everything so hard, man? My friends don't get it and Mum's not here. Would *Kesia* get it? It wasn't that bad working with her on the project. Kesia knows a lot – even though she still thinks she's better than me, but . . . she's all right. I don't mind working with her.

Time slips away and before I know it Dad hovers over me. 'Isaiah, it's time to go.'

He doesn't wait for me, so I hurry after him to keep up. 'What did they say?'

'It doesn't matter,' Dad mutters, tension locking his back and shoulders as we leave the centre.

'Dad, come on. Tell me what they said. It can't have been that bad.'

'Isaiah, it's not about what they said,' he says after a while. 'I could tell the assessor thought I was exaggerating. How can I "prove" that I can't walk properly or work properly? The pain comes and goes. How can I prove that I'm in pain sometimes and I have no ways to control it? I don't know when a flare-up will happen. As if I would make this pain up! Now I can't even provide for my son!'

I try to give Dad a sideways hug, but he winces in pain.

'You said "can't" is not a part of our vocabulary,' I reply. 'You won't know until you get the decision letter back.'

Uncle Kwame's name flashes on Dad's phone screen, but he silences the call. It's the first time I've ever seen him do that.

'You didn't see the assessor's face, Isaiah.' Dad scowls. 'It's the same expression I see everywhere – even on our landlord's face. I *know* that look. They don't believe me. They think I'm workshy.' Tension drains from Dad's body almost like he can't keep his body up any more. 'Let's just go home. I'm tired.'

Dad huddles on the sofa with the hot-water bottle and canned tomato soup I heated up steaming the air. Dad's phone pings with a message from his boss.

'What was that call yesterday before the arcade? I know you didn't wanna tell me when I was with my friends.'

'It's my fault.' Dad's fingers rub at his forehead. 'I told you before that Rick asked if I could cover a few extra hours when people were off sick. I thought . . . yes, maybe I can get that money before the landlord comes hounding us again.'

'That's good,' I reply, relaxing on the lumpy sofa beside him.

'Unfortunately, those few hours were seen as an "increased wage" and the Universal Credit we get was reduced for this month.'

My body is as stiff as an ironing board. 'So we have even *less* money? How are we gonna pay the landlord?'

'I will deal with him,' he replies glumly. 'It's just for this month. We can manage. People are buying my woodwork products when I can make them.'

We're not even *managing* now.

Ding. Ding. Ding.

'I have to meet a friend quickly . . . for school.'

Dad frowns at me. 'It's getting dark. Can't you meet with them another time?'

'Oh . . . uh . . . my friend lives in the block.'

'Is it Kesia?' Dad asks. 'She's the one you're doing the history exhibition with? She lives on the bottom floor with her parents if I remember correctly.'

If she still wants to do the exhibition. 'No, it's someone else, but I promise not to be late.'

Moving down the stairs to the basement, I pause at the black bins to pick some rubbish that will burn. The handle to the basement isn't hot this time.

I throw rubbish into the fireplace, settling into my makeshift seat. Jacob appears in the fireplace with the same bruise on his cheek and split lip. 'Are you all right, Jacob? Who were those guys beating you up?'

'You saw that happen? Those barbarians. I was attempting to make some money by singing, but they didn't appreciate me

150

stealing their "prime" location street corner. I was saved by Felix.'

A ratty white boy with jet-black hair appears near Jacob in the fireplace. *'Ya done your work yet?'*

Felix swipes dust from the fireplace, chasing Jacob with his grimy finger, but I can see he's joking with him.

'Keep away.' Jacob laughs breathlessly. *'Yes, I'm almost done. I will come and find you once I've finished.'*

Felix rubs the dirt on to his trousers. *'Save you a seat at supper.'* He moves away.

'Felix saved me from those thugs on the street and I told him my story. He's agreed to help.'

My mouth loosens. 'I thought you said that the other kids there were "apathetic". I googled that and it means they're uninterested.'

'Well, what can I say?' he replies with a wry grin, sweeping the fireplace. *'I've probably inhaled too much soot or you're rubbing off on me. I do still believe they could do with some etiquette training. They chew with their mouths open.'*

I laugh. 'Did you get my letter? Did you go to William Webster?'

Jacob picks up an apron with the WW logo on it and I cheer. *'After failing at street performance, I went there as you suggested. Mr Webster saw I was a terrible shop keep, but realised I was wonderful with words and excel at counting, particularly, and so he offered me a* job! *The money is a pittance, but I can save up enough to get to Manchester and find my father's acquaintance.'*

I smile back. 'You're a big step closer.'

'As a thank you, I have brought you a gift from the store. Mr Webster said I could choose one item. It's only small, but maybe you can display it at your history presentation. I'll leave it in the fire.'

He places a green glass bottle labelled 'Brimstone and Treacle' on the hearthstone. 'Is that poison?'

Jacob throws his hands up. *'No, Isaiah. Brimstone and Treacle is a type of medicine. Why don't you "google it"?'*

'I will! And I don't know if I'm even doing that presentation any more. Kesia doesn't want to do it with me.'

'Kesia.' I can feel Jacob's eyes on me, burning through the fire. *'Did you behave improperly towards a lady, Isaiah?'*

I push up from my makeshift seat. 'No, I didn't! And Kesia isn't some *lady*. She's just Kesia. If she thinks she can do the presentation without me, I don't even care.'

'It seems like you do care.'

'There's stuff going on and she was . . . I don't even know why she got so angry. And now I don't think she's even talking to me.'

And as I admit that I realise that's the last thing I want. I need Kesia's help.

'Why don't you tell her about all this "stuff" going on?'

I grunt.

'If I had not met you through the fire, what would I have done? Succumbed to a slow and painful death in this horrible workhouse. This ghastly experience has taught me to live each day as though it's your last and appreciate the good people, however uncivilised, around you.'

Uncivilised. I laugh.

'Have you heard any other news about my father?'

'Not yet, but I'm gonna need more help.'

Chapter Twenty-Five

Monday

'I swear on my mum's life, Isaiah. The next time we go to the arcade, I'm gonna beat both of you at Kart Racing Extreme,' Fredrick remarks, slamming the door to his school locker.

'Not on your mum's life.' Kieran chuckles.

I haven't seen Kesia all day at school, but I know she's in.

'Who are you looking for?' Kieran asks.

'No one,' I reply instantly, facing forward, but that makes Kieran even more suspicious as he looks around too.

'Isaiah, there you are,' Mrs Morris says, the frown lines around her mouth showing she means business. 'I need to speak with you.'

'Hi, miss.' I force a smile, the muscles straining in my cheeks. 'We've got history now.'

'I won't keep you for too long,' she replies, not backing down. 'Gentlemen, off to your lesson, please.'

Kieran lifts his chin, motioning to Fredrick. 'We're Isaiah's friends.'

'Yeah,' Fredrick says. 'We wanna know too.'

Mrs Morris takes a calculated step towards them. 'I'm very aware that you are both Isaiah's friends and Isaiah can tell you anything he wants once I have this meeting with him and his father. Alone.'

'My dad . . . is here?' Today is one of his working days, which means he's missing work to be here. 'I'll see you in history,' I say to Kieran and Fredrick.

Mrs Morris waits for my friends to leave. 'I called your father to follow up on the letter I sent home. He was happy to come in and discuss with me. I'll lead the way.'

'Your letter must've got lost in the post,' I say. 'You know how these things are.'

'Hmmm, I do know indeed.' Mrs Morris hums, opening her office door for me. Dad waits in the chair.

'Hi, son.'

I can't tell if he's upset. 'Hi, Dad.'

Mrs Morris doesn't sit down at her desk but leans on it to face Dad and me, so it doesn't feel as official.

'I won't keep you long, Mr Oni. I know you need to get back to work soon. I called an official meeting because we've noticed that in the year Isaiah has been here he's been late several times or absent. Isaiah is an otherwise *exceptional* student, but his punctuality and attendance is concerning, especially as it'll affect any awards he might receive at the end of the school year. We want to work with you to help improve this.'

'I can explain,' Dad responds immediately. 'Sometimes Isaiah helps me around the house here and there, but it's not a cause for concern. Isaiah will not miss school again or be late. You have my word.'

My stomach hardens. Dad can't always control what his body does or when his pain comes even though I know he wishes he could.

'Is that true, Isaiah?' Mrs Morris asks, facing me.

'Yeah, like my dad said,' I agree. 'I won't be late or anything like that again.'

Another lie. Who else can help Dad?

'If there's nothing else to say, then we will leave this for now.' Mrs Morris scribbles some things down on a form and shakes Dad's hand. 'And if there are ever any concerns about Isaiah that you'd like to discuss, I am here to help. Isaiah has been a great addition to this school.'

'I agree,' Dad says, holding on softly to the back of my neck. 'I'm so proud of him.'

'Isaiah, you're free to go back to your lesson now,' Mrs Morris says. 'I want to have a quick word with your dad here before he leaves for work.'

I close the door and go to history.

Mrs Morris should leave it alone.

'What percentage of people in Britain live in poverty today?' Mr Paterson asks. 'Can you guess?'

Everyone who answers gets it wrong.

Kesia would've known the answer to this but she's not here.

'The answer is twenty-two per cent.'

'That's not *that* much!' Fredrick speaks.

'You would think so, but twenty-two per cent is actually 14.5 million people.' Mr Paterson pauses to watch the stunned expressions around the room. 'That is one in five people. Just think about that every time you're in a group.'

Fredrick looks around the classroom, nudging me. 'Who do you think is poor here?'

I can *never* tell my friends about me.

'What did Mr Morris want with you and your dad?' Kieran asks, copying down notes from the board.

'Nothing. It's because I've been late and miss school sometimes.'

'Workhouses were also known as "prisons of the poor". We're going to be looking in depth at workhouses today. I have stuck sources around the room about them. You're to go to each station and take notes. You have ten minutes only. Go!'

My friends race off to the different stations, but I don't get up and instead stay working on the exhibition project.

Letters from a Victorian boy
    Profile: Jacob comes from a wealthy background, but he ended up in Cricklewood Workhouse. His uncle left him there after Jacob's dad went missing. Jacob wants to escape, but he has no money. Jacob got a job to get to Manchester, where one of his dad's friends lives. The railway system is still being set up. The workhouse conditions are bad and Jacob isn't treated fairly by the guardian. I think that Jacob's rich background and mixed heritage might have something to do with how he's being treated.
    The letters are between me (a boy in the present) with Jacob (a boy in the past). We're connected through the building we both live in. My estate used to be Cricklewood Workhouse.

'Hard at work, Isaiah?' Mr Paterson says. 'How is the

exhibition prep going? I know you like to do things alone, but I hope you're working together with Kesia. Her brain is like a computer, you know.'

I hesitate.

'The dream needs to work as a team to be a dream team.'

I burst out laughing and Mr Paterson laughs with me.

'Do you know why Kesia isn't in today?' I ask.

'That I do not.'

Chapter Twenty-Six

I think about what Jacob said about the people that help you.

Me: you missed history

Kesia: I know

'Are you coming to lunch?' Kieran asks, glancing at my phone screen to see who I'm texting. 'Are you and Kesia really friends?'

Me: I have something to tell you
It's important

Kesia is typing

Kesia: I'm in the sensory room

I ignore his question. 'Why don't I come and meet you in the canteen later?' I say before Kieran can stop me.

I knock on the door of the sensory room. After a while I hear the handle turning and Kesia's face appears.

'I've never been inside the sensory room before,' I say awkwardly, stepping into a different world.

The air feels cooler in here. Calming music plays in the background with LED lights brightening the room. The coloured blobs in the lava lamps bob up and down. Bean bags are spread out around the room. I dive on to one as Kesia settles back on an orange yoga mat similar to Dad's.

'You come in here to do yoga or something?' I ask.

Using a small remote, Kesia switches off the music and answers me. 'Yes. What did you want to tell me?'

I jump up off the bean bag and run to play with one of the lights. 'Why?'

'Yoga is good for relaxation. Stress means more pain for me.' Kesia's open palm thumps on to the mat. 'Can you stop touching things?'

I stop what I'm doing. 'They said yoga would help my dad with his back pain, but he's not into it, so we do stretches instead.'

'It's different for everyone. What did you want to tell me?'

Sitting back down on the bean bag, I can feel the itchy material through my trousers.

'Isaiah, what do you want?' she asks.

I can't avoid it any more. I have to tell her.

'I came to say that I'm sorry for treating you like I don't need you for the project. Like I don't need you for anything. You were just trying to help.' I offer her a scrunched piece of tissue. Kesia squints at the tissue in my open hand. 'It's for you.'

She peels back the folds of the tissue, revealing a wriggling woodlouse I found in the field.

She smiles. 'I love bugs.' She carefully takes the tissue from my hand. 'I'll release her back outside later.' Kesia leans forward on her mat. 'So what else did you find out about *Roman's Chance*?'

'It was shipwrecked in the English Channel. But it didn't say where the survivors were taken.'

'I bet they brought them back to England.' Kesia rests her feet on either thigh in a stretch. 'And put them in a hospital here.'

'Hospitals! Duh. Why didn't I think to check there?' I ask myself.

Kesia changes into an eagle pose. 'But there weren't any proper hospital records until after 1850. They didn't always keep accurate documentation of all the patients in those days.'

'So you're saying we won't find him?'

'Not necessarily. There are a few hospitals around England that have digital archives of records from the early eighteen hundreds. Do you have a picture of the missing man? If his name isn't listed, we could try to identify him by his features.'

It's only Kesia that will know this kind of stuff.

I'll ask Jacob. 'I'll find out.'

I smirk. 'I *knew* you'd want to work together again.'

'We're not.' Kesia rolls up her mat. 'You can't talk your way out of everything, Isaiah. We were supposed to be a team.'

I thought she was back in for sure.

'Why were you pushing me away?' she asks.

I don't say anything. She stands with the mat tucked under her arm, turning.

'Wait!' The words are lost at first, but I find them before she reaches the door. 'There's some stuff going on, but I haven't told anyone about it – not even my friends. I *do* wanna work with you again. I swear . . .'

'And you promise you won't be like before?'

'I swear it.'

'When do you want to meet next?'

Chapter Twenty-Seven

Uncle Kwame parts the last section of my hair into a wave so my cornrows will swerve. The barbershop is quiet today and only the hum of the music fills up the silence.

'How are you, young blood?' he says, oiling my scalp.

'I'm all right, Unc. Sorry I ran out without fixing the chairs. I'll finish them today.' *Because we really need the money.*

'We're good. They're still in the corner,' Uncle Kwame responds, plaiting the end of the last cornrow. 'All done.'

I move my head from side to side in the mirror, admiring my hair. 'These are fresh. Thanks.'

I settle down in the corner of the barbershop, taking out the instructions again and all the chair parts. I'm here for a few hours. When I'm finished, we slide the chairs over.

'This boy can do anything,' Uncle Kwame praises me, and even swivels around in the chair for extra effect.

He turns to the barbershop, addressing everyone. 'Do

you know how smart this boy is? He's going to be the next big tech billionaire; you mark my words. He's already representing his school.'

Uncle Kwame takes out his brown leather wallet from his pocket and removes £50, much more than I expected.

'Here you go.' He slaps the money into my palm as our hands connect. 'Buy whatever you want. No questions asked.'

'Thanks, Uncle Kwame.' I don't have enough for our landlord, but at least I can give him something. Raising my voice, I address the whole shop. 'If you need anything fixed or put together, I can do it all. Barbershop discount included.' I add the last part, remembering what Mr Lim said.

'Now, tell me, who doesn't love a discount?' Mr Lim asked. *'Even if people know it's not really a discount, they'll still take it.'*

When I reach my estate, I bump into Clarice, who carries a box up the stairs with G.M. hopping up by her side.

'Isaiah.' She pauses with the box, shifting it to rest on her hip.

I point to it. 'Do you need help with that?'

Clarice grunts, lifting the box up and down like she's a bodybuilder. 'I've been carrying art supplies on my own for *years*, but I do have a job for you. Are you free this week? I don't want to interfere too much with your schoolwork.'

'Yeah, and this is kinda part of my schoolwork. Did you finish the painting for the gallery yet?'

'You have a great memory. Yes, I did finish that painting, but I have even more to do because I have a new exhibition coming up in a few weeks. I'll be home most days after four. Just knock. See you soon.'

I walk into the flat as Dad shouts at someone on the phone.

'I don't know why Mrs Morris called you too!'

'Because I'm his mother!' Mum shouts back through the phone. *'Matthew, why is Isaiah missing school and why is he always late? I thought you got a handle on things.'*

'What like my disability? Yes, I'll get a handle on that right away.'

'You told me that you'll be able to look after Isaiah despite what happened. You wanted him with you instead of him moving to Berlin with me.'

'You're studying, Amma!' Dad shouts. 'You wouldn't have had the proper time for Isaiah and you know it. Don't put this all on me.'

'You didn't say I could come with you, Mum,' I speak.

Dad turns slowly, seeing me at the door. 'When did you get in?'

'Isaiah.' Mum pauses, probably rubbing at her temples. *'I proposed the idea of you coming to Berlin with me to your father,*

but he wanted to keep you in the UK. He wanted to keep you somewhere familiar.'

Somewhere familiar. Somewhere with family.

If we hadn't moved here, I wouldn't have met any of my friends, but then I would've been with Mum. I *never* get to see her.

Chapter Twenty-Eight

Tuesday

'It's independent working on your sites today,' Mr Iyer says. 'For those who want to know how to add hyperlinks, please look at the board now.' *Sniff.* 'This is so the visitors to your website can move around. If you already know how to do this, you can get on with it. Please make a note of everything you're doing and all the decisions made for the assessment section later on.'

Slumped in a rotating chair, I spin one way and then the other.

'I proposed the idea of you coming to Berlin with me to your father.' I couldn't imagine moving away from Shepten when Dad and my friends are here. I'd see Mum every day, but everything else would be different. My life would be different.

'Kieran, Darius's mum and dad are divorced, yeah?' I ask suddenly.

'Uh, yeah. They're divorced. Why are you asking?' he replies.

Kesia's eyes meet mine through the gap in the computers and she mouths, *Are you OK?*

I half shake my head and turn to Kieran. 'No reason. Do you still want help with your website?'

'Yeah, you need to show me the HTML thing again.' Kieran talks rapidly. 'I *thought* I did it right, but some of my pages aren't loading properly. Why do you find it easy? It's hard.'

Clicking, I scroll down Kieran's homepage. 'It's not loading properly because you forgot the end tags. Remember what Mr Iyer was saying about tags working in pairs. It's like when you open a door, you have to close it, yeah?'

'I get it. So if I put that tag at the end, there won't be any errors?'

'Do that and refresh the page.'

I point out exactly where the tags are missing and Kieran adds them in.

'Thanks, Isaiah,' Kieran says. 'I drew some logos for your business.' He slides a piece of paper over. 'You can pick which one you like the best.'

A smile builds on my face as I look at the different designs. 'These are dope.'

Kieran shrugs. 'You always help me when I need help so it's cool. Looked like you needed help, anyways.'

'What do you mean?' I ask, thinking that he's been noticing things like Uncle Kwame has.

'Why do you look scared, man?' Kieran jokes, nudging my shoulder. 'I wanted to help. When you go around with Darius, the logos would be cool on business cards.'

'Thanks. I like this one best.' I point to the logo with 'Matthew' in large font and 'Sons' in a smaller font with a hammer at the top.

'I can't wait for your birthday party, Kieran,' Kirsty says, popping up between the computer screens.

Fredrick smiles at her. 'We get to choose the food we want too. I'm going to get rice and peas, jerk chicken, mac and cheese – all of it.'

While Mr Iyer is teaching about hyperlinks at the front, more people turn towards us, asking Kieran about his epic party. It's getting more exaggerated every time anyone talks about it.

Ignoring them, I click through my website, adding in discount offers like Mr Lim suggested.

I hear the faint clock tower bells chiming in the distance. *Ding. Ding. Ding.*

The room changes around me and projects the Victorian hospital, flickering black and white. People cough and groan. One of the nurses checks on the same man with the bandages on his head.

'How are you feeling today, sir?' she asks, pouring him a glass of water and picking up something white from the floor. 'I believe you dropped your handkerchief. I will put it up here for safekeeping—'

'No,' he cries out, turning in his bed. 'Give it to me, please.'

The classroom goes back to normal as Kieran talks about his dad.

'He's back from Thailand and he bought me some strawberry sweets. They're insanely sugary.' He hands them out discreetly, with Fredrick watching for Mr Iyer. 'I got whole packs for you guys.'

I pocket it knowing Mr Lim would like some because he loves anything sweet. 'Thanks.'

'Look at what else my dad got me,' Kieran says, showing me and Fredrick a picture of his galaxy-style hand-drawn customised Nikes. 'It's a Haruto original. My dad stopped in Japan to get these especially for me. Haruto was doing a pop up.'

'These are too clean.' I look at the screen and my jaw tightens. 'They probably sell for as much as that drone Mum's sending me.'

Why did I talk about that stupid drone again? It still hasn't showed up. My birthday was ages ago.

'When you get all that money from your business, you can buy any ones you like,' Kieran suggests.

'Attention back to your websites.'

After school there is a small queue outside the food bank and it takes ages for me to reach Reggie.

'Same as usual?' Reggie asks, holding up a used Sainsbury's bag. 'Oh, and I saved these magazines especially for you. Kesia mentioned that you like tech.'

Reggie pulls out a few copies of *Techno Digest* from underneath the desk and hands them to me.

'I don't need them – just the food.'

'You didn't stay long at the arcade. Will you come again next time?'

'Uh, yeah. Maybe.'

'I'm going to just leave these magazines here – in case you change your mind.'

Reggie goes to pack the bag and I glance at the stack of magazines on the counter. *I could read one.*

'How many ways can you create life from a vegetable?' I say to myself, reading the first page.

Kesia lifts a sack of oranges on to the end of the table.

'One day I'm gonna be inside the magazine as an inventor,' I say, mostly to myself.

'Here you go,' Reggie says, handing me the full bag. He notices the magazine in my hand. 'I guess Kesia was right.'

I look up and see she's shooting a rare smile over my way. I grin back.

Chapter Twenty-Nine

I drop off the food at home, making sure everything is in the right cupboards. 'Dad, I got the shopping.'

I have to quickly see Jacob before I meet Darius. I need to tell him what Kesia thought of.

'Dad?'

He doesn't reply.

I come out of the kitchen with a packet of rice in my hand. 'Dad?'

Dad's face tweaks in pain as he perches on the edge of the sofa. 'I should've known that he was backing off too easy.'

'Who?'

He has a letter in his hands.

'Is that another letter from school?' I ask, putting the rice down on the table. 'I haven't been late.'

'It's not you. It's the landlord.' Dad groans, rubbing his left leg. 'He didn't even come here himself to tell me. If he wants a fight, I'll give him one.' Dad tosses the letter down on the table as he grabs his phone to make a call in the bathroom.

My eyes find the important parts of the letter.

EVICTION NOTICE
2 WEEKS

'But his deadline wasn't until tomorrow!'

All the work I did was for nothing.

Ding. Ding. Ding.

The clock tower bells chime and I slam the letter back on the table, send a text to Dad to tell him I've gone out and rush down the stairs.

It's automatic now. I throw the paper in, waiting for the fire and Jacob to appear, but instead there's a torn piece of newspaper inside.

Dear Isaiah,

Many things have happened since we spoke last. I had Felix drop off this letter in the fireplace because I'm under punishment from the cruel Mr Moore. I questioned the insanitary and dangerous conditions of the workhouse and he locked me in a store cupboard all day for questioning him. It's bad enough that he locks us in our dormitory every night — the cupboard was tiny and I could feel the weevils crawling all over me.

Jacob needs to get out of there.

If anyone speaks out, we get punished or disappear completely. More and more children are going missing each day. I heard that he's selling them off to work in factories. They try to starve us, so we won't have enough energy to complain. I have to do something. I'm going to be wiser like you. Braver.

If I was wise, we wouldn't be becoming homeless — again.

If I can get enough people here to fight against Mr Moore, we can stop him. You're always telling me to act rather than complain so I must.
    Best,
    Jacob

Dear Jacob,

I'm glad you're doing something about Mr Moore but be safe. Things have been changing here too. Our landlord says he's going to kick us out of the flat we're living in for missed rent payments, but Dad thinks it's more than that and so do I. I thought I could raise the money we owe, but he sent us an eviction letter, which means we're being kicked out of our home. I didn't want to tell you. But if you're not giving up, then I'm not giving up too.

Do you have a photo of your dad or can you describe him to me? We're thinking he might be in a hospital recovering somewhere.

Isaiah

I throw the letter in the fire and my phone goes off.

Darius: I'm downstairs. Where are you?

'What do you think?' I ask Mr Lim as he scrolls through the Matthew & Sons site. 'I'm still missing some things, but I'm working on it.'

I mount another picture frame on the wall for Mr Lim, making it the fourth one. 'Is this position—'

Mr Lim raises one hand to stop me. 'It's good. But we can make it better.'

'Really?' I ask, leaning back to look at all the neatly positioned picture frames. 'But it's straight.'

'No, no. The picture frames are good. I meant your website.'

'Better? How?' I ask. 'If there's something to add, I would have added it already. I did everything you said.'

'Darius, you're a music man. How long does it take you to perfect a song?'

Darius swallows some of Mrs Lim's spicy roast chicken, deflating his cheeks. 'It takes however long it takes, but when it feels right, then I go with it.'

'Good.' Mr Lim nods. 'There's always more to do.'

Darius holds up a finger. 'I didn't exactly say that—'

Mr Lim interrupts him. 'Where is the contact form? If a customer has an issue, how are they supposed to contact you?'

'They can just tell me if they've got problems when I visit.'

'What if the problem happens later? And this isn't the correct font or colour. I told you that it's important to know your customer.'

'I *do* know my customer,' I insist. 'People who want me to fix things for them.'

I know my website is already better than most people's in my class.

'It's more than that,' Mr Lim explains. 'It's for adults who are either unable to fix things themselves or they don't have the time to. Think about why they need you. It's about building a brand. Go with bright and sharp colours. It's bold, it's assured and it shows a confident business. I will demonstrate.'

Mr Lim puts two websites side by side. 'Does one of the sites make you feel a certain way?'

I point to the one on the left. 'This one is calmer and this one feels . . . like, more . . . energetic.'

'Good, good,' Mr Lim replies. 'This will get you extra marks for thinking bigger.'

'I'll make the changes, thanks.'

'Good.' Mr Lim slams the lid of the laptop down and fishes his leather wallet out of his coat. 'You're a fine worker.'

He slips two twenty-pound notes into my hand.

'Thanks, Mr Lim.'

Even though the landlord sent that eviction letter, I can't give up now. We leave Mr Lim's house.

'Darius, can I ask you a question?' I speak. 'What's it like with your parents being divorced?'

'It's . . .' He pauses, thinking of the word. 'Different.'

'Is it better?'

'It's different,' Darius repeats, laughing at the look on my face. 'My parents weren't happy together, so it was easier once they were apart.'

'My parents have been separated for years. I'm used to it now. I thought I wouldn't care now they're getting divorced.'

'But you do a little?'

I nod. 'And it's not just that. They get to make all these big decisions about who you live with and when you get to see them.'

'When my parents divorced, my dad moved away too. Why don't you speak to your parents and tell them what you're thinking? I haven't met your mum, but if she's as cool as your dad, then she'll want to know.'

Will she?

Chapter Thirty

Wednesday

Water drips from Mr Paterson's head as fake sweat and he groans, clutching his stomach in pain. Everyone leans back as he coughs into a tissue.

'Today we're looking at public health and hygiene in the nineteenth century.' Mr Paterson groans again, wiping his forehead. 'What infection do you think I have?'

I take in all the symptoms: sweating, pain in the stomach and the coughing. These are the symptoms Jacob said his mum had before she passed away.

'TB,' I say.

Mr Paterson straightens up, pointing at me with his germy tissue. 'Yes, Isaiah. It is indeed TB, or tuberculosis if you want to be fancy. TB is a bacterial infection which killed many in the eighteenth and nineteenth centuries. Why? Can anyone guess?'

Kesia's hand is straight up next, waving around like she's signalling a plane. Mr Paterson chooses her.

'Because there was no cure for it yet.'

'This is indeed part of it. Another major factor in the spread of infectious diseases was the overcrowded living conditions and poor sanitation of those living conditions. Between 1851 and 1910, around four million people died from TB. In fact, within the last decade or so, London has had a resurgence of TB cases due to overcrowding. In the nineteenth century, it was believed that diseases were caused by direct exposure to filth and decay and so things like "bad smells" were the culprit.' Mr Paterson brings up a black-and-white image of people washing the streets with a hose. 'How does disease link in with washing the streets?'

'Uh, is it that they thought that if they washed the streets, there wouldn't be diseases any more? I'm not sure, sir,' says Kirsty.

'Bingo. The people in the image were cleaning the streets of London to prevent the spread of cholera, another infectious virus. There was a huge outbreak of the virus in the nineteenth century. We're going to gather information on the key people who helped to change public health. I have set up the sources around the classroom. Pair up with your surname sibling again.'

'We're together then, Fredrick,' Kieran says. 'I bet we'll beat you both.'

'No, we're gonna win,' Kesia fires back, appearing beside us. 'Come on, Isaiah. We're wasting time.'

'Healthy competition – that's what I like to hear.' Mr Paterson punches his fist into the air. 'I want you to note down: Who they were? What was the problem before they came along? What did they do/build/discover/invent or change? Once you have all of that, you will decide how significant their discovery was. Go!'

Fredrick trips over his bag as he runs across the room.

'I don't want to explain to the headteacher and your parents why you broke your neck in my history class, Fredrick. Slow down.'

Kesia points to two different sources at the back of the classroom. 'You do Edward Jenner and I'll do Louis Pasteur.'

Edward Jenner – In 1796 Edward Jenner discovered how to vaccinate against one of Britain's worst diseases – smallpox.

Louis Pasteur – Pasteur was a French scientist who in 1861 discovered that tiny microbes (bacteria) caused disease.

We spend the next fifteen minutes moving swiftly around the classroom, mainly to beat Kieran and Fredrick.

'I can't even read your writing, Fredrick,' Kieran cries, shaking his book. 'It's just scribbles. Can *you* even read your own writing?'

It looks like cats attacked Fredrick's history book.

'It doesn't matter! We still got all the notes down first!'

'Now, with your partner, I want you to look at all the information you collected and decide which was the most significant in improving the health of the public. Only those with good answers will be let off ten minutes earlier for lunch so make them great.'

'Let's go with Joseph Lister,' Kesia says. 'Many people died after operations back then because of infections and, if it wasn't for him using the antiseptic spray . . .'

'. . . and getting people to wash their hands, more people would've died,' I finish. 'Yeah, let's write the paragraph on Lister.'

'Next lesson, we're going to look a few years on and discuss some other public health changes that happened, including sewers, public toilets and access to clean water. Pack away, class. You all deserve those ten minutes!' Mr Paterson bellows over the clattering sound of chairs.

'Public library after school?' Kesia asks. 'We have *a lot* to do.'

I raise my eyebrow. 'I *do* have other stuff to do, you know.'

'Like what? I thought you wanted to win. If you want to win then—'

'All right. I'll see you after school.' *Does she live there or something?*

Chapter Thirty-One

'These letters are great, Isaiah,' Kesia praises me.

'Of course they'll be great. It's *me* we're talking about,' I comment, and Kesia rolls her eyes, but a smile peeks through.

'They feel really real. How did you get the language correct? And the details?'

A smile slips on to my face. 'Now, why would I share all my secrets? But I *can* tell you that I have a special source who knows a thing or two about the nineteenth century.'

'We'll have the edge on the other teams for sure. Let me show you the map of Shepton I've been working on.'

She's designed it on her computer with animations and everything. When you click on a red dot on the map, a paragraph comes up, explaining what it used to be and what it is now.

'There are *loads* of places that used to be other things back in the day.'

'My uncle Kwame's shop used to be a convenience store called William Webster.'

'Is that so? Do you think your uncle will talk to us about his barbershop and its history? I thought it would be cool to interview the people in these places now. We can ask if they know what the building used to be and what it means to them now. The judges are going to love it.'

It's kind of cool when someone is *that* into something. Kesia points to each red dot on the map, explaining what she has so far. 'Did you know that the local assessment centre used to be an asylum?'

'What?'

'Yeah,' Kesia replies, flipping through her notes. 'It used to be the Shepten Asylum. It wasn't the nicest of places.'

It still isn't. Dad should be receiving his assessment decision any day now. Even though he pretends to forget about it, I see him staring at the post when it comes every morning.

'Quiet down, please,' the librarian says to a group tucked in the corner of the library.

'Are you listening, Isaiah?'

'Yeah, we're going to need more people for the interviews. Why don't we ask the librarian?'

'That's a good idea,' she exclaims. 'I'll go and ask her now.'

When Kesia leaves, I think more about Jacob. There

wasn't a letter back in the fireplace today. I hope he isn't still on punishment with Mr Moore. I scroll through more hospital records online.

Kesia returns. 'She's helping someone, but she has some free time after. Have you found anything in the records about the missing man from the shipwreck?'

'I wrote down a list of hospitals that we have to call. They don't give access online for some of their older records, even with Mr Paterson's card. We can use the library phone when it's free.'

'We?' Kesia grins. 'And did you manage to find any photograph of him?'

'Uh, not yet. Quick, the phone is free.'

Hurrying across the library, I slide into the booth and hold the door open for Kesia. We slip in before an older woman gets there; she taps on the glass door, her dark, narrowing eyes locked on us like magnets. I flash her one of my smiles and she moves away.

'She *really* wanted to use the phone.'

We try so many hospitals. Some don't pick up and others have no records or they need more information before they can help us. Some tell us they don't have time to help a bunch of kids with endless questions.

I slam the phone down after the last call. 'What a waste of time.'

'No, it wasn't because we've narrowed down which ones it could be. Do you get how great this will be for the exhibition? A *real* mystery from the past.'

What she doesn't know is that the past is really my present.

'Have you kids finished?' the old woman asks, banging on the door. 'The sign says max half an hour!'

We leave the booth and she closes the glass door behind her, puffing. The librarian beckons us over and puts up a 'Be right back' sign.

'We can go to the quiet area of the library,' she says, leading us through the bookshelves.

'Do you tell yourself to be quiet when you make noise?' I ask her, and Kesia giggles behind me.

'No, of course not,' the librarian replies, tightening her lips. 'That would be preposterous.'

Preposterous sounds like a word Jacob would use. We sink into the plush blue chairs in the corner of the library and Kesia has her notebook ready. I have my phone ready too.

'What would you like to ask me? My name is Penelope, by the way. You're researching for your history exhibition project?'

'Yeah,' Kesia replies. 'We're asking people around the local area about its history and their connection to it. Do you know anything about the library's history?'

'You probably have guessed that this was a clock tower,

but not many people know that it wasn't just for telling the time,' she explains. 'It was essential for warning townspeople of emergencies, like when that huge fire ripped through Shepten in 1838. Madame Danvers, the town's benefactor, then rebuilt this building.'

'What fire?' I ask.

The librarian leans forward like she's sharing a secret with us. 'In 1838, a fire started at Cricklewood Workhouse. The fire consumed *everything*. This clock tower alerted people and the community responded. Wait here.'

The librarian disappears between the shelves to get something.

'Can you believe it?' Kesia speaks. 'A great fire here in Shepten.'

The librarian reappears, flipping through the pages of a dense book, until she reaches a particular page. She places it down on the table in between us.

It's a black-and-white picture of Cricklewood Workhouse and it's on fire. The flames roar up the sides of the building with smoke pouring out of the windows. Half of the workhouse has collapsed as people rush to get out, scared.

'They managed to put the fire out, but Cricklewood Workhouse was permanently closed after that. It probably would've been closed down regardless because of the complaints of mistreatment.'

I try to process everything the librarian has said. 'I don't understand. Why didn't I know there was a fire there before?'

'Because Shepten was revived by Madame Rosalind Danvers. She even restored the workhouse building but decreed that it should never serve as a workhouse again.'

'When in 1838 was the fire?' I ask. 'What caused it?'

'Around the 8th April 1838, but they never found out what caused the blaze.'

This is the reason why I can see Jacob, isn't it? Jacob is going to die in that fire without ever finding his father unless I stop it happening.

'Good luck with your project.' The librarian takes the heavy book back to the shelf, leaving us alone.

'I have to try and prevent the fire,' I say under my breath.

Dad said you don't have an encounter for no reason.

Maybe I've just found out mine.

'What do you mean, you have to try and prevent the fire?' Kesia asks, fixing the bobby pin in her afro. 'You can't stop a fire that's already happened, Isaiah.'

I slam my palm on the table. 'But it *hasn't* happened yet – not really.'

Kesia leans closer to me, lowering her voice, 'Are you all right? That fire happened in 1838. It's 2023.'

'You're not gonna believe me if I told you.'

She raises her chin. 'Believe what?'

'Come with me, I'll show you.'

Chapter Thirty-Two

I wait outside the basement for Kesia. She had to go and drop her stuff at home. Is she going to come back? If it was the other way around, I wouldn't come back either. Who would listen to someone going on about changing things that had already happened in the past?

A video-call notification comes up on my phone. I accept Mum's call.

The background is dark with only a glow on Mum's face like she's telling a spooky ghost story.

'*Isaiah, you answered.*' She yawns, squeezing her eyes shut and then opening them wide. She blinks.

'Why are you so tired? Isn't it only six p.m. in Berlin?'

Mum yawns again. '*Yes, but I stayed up all night studying and work has been busy. But this call isn't about me. Your father and I should have spoken to you properly about the whole moving to Berlin situation. You shouldn't have found out that way.*'

'Mum, if I'm being honest, I wouldn't have wanted to move to Berlin.'

Mum doesn't say anything for a few seconds, only staring through the screen before looking down. *'We never get to see each other, Isaiah. If you did come now, we could spend more time together.'*

'I wanna see you, Mum, but I don't wanna leave Shepten. And you're studying too. I wouldn't wanna get in the way.'

'Isaiah, you would never be in the way. It seems like you're struggling there with your father,' Mum replies, ignoring how hard she is making this for me. *'Just . . . just don't make any hasty decisions, OK? I just want what's best for you. Speak to you soon.'*

'Bye, Mum,' I say.

'What did you want to show me?' Kesia asks from beside me.

I swallow the squeal. *When did she get here?*

A sly smile twists Kesia's face. 'Did I scare you this time? I did, didn't I?'

'No, you didn't.' I pull on the basement door to get away from her teasing.

'If you say so . . . whoa . . .' Kesia creeps in. 'This is like stepping back in time!'

I pause in front of the fireplace, cracking my knuckles. 'I'm not sure what you're gonna be able to see.'

'Okaaay.' Kesia watches as I throw an old newspaper inside the fireplace and wait for the strange flame to appear.

It bursts to life.

'Whoa, I've never seen a flame that colour before,' Kesia exclaims.

'Wait for it.'

Jacob appears after a few seconds and I'm happy to see he's fine.

'Good afternoon, Isaiah, and am I having the pleasure of making Kesia's acquaintance?'

'Whoa!' Kesia exclaims again. 'How can we see . . . is that a workhouse? Is there a mirror back there? Wait. Is it *this* workhouse?'

'Uh-huh. Kesia, what else can you see?' I ask, dying to know the answer.

'I can see a room . . . no, a dormitory with lots of beds crowded together.' Kesia's mouth falls open.

'And that's it?'

'What else am I supposed to see? That's incredible! How long have you been able to see this?'

'You can't see the boy in the fireplace?'

'I'm not a boy. I'm a distinguished young man. What is it that she's saying?' Jacob bows.

'Why are you bowing? She can't even see you.'

195

'Isaiah, who are you talking to?' Kesia says.

'Or hear you, apparently.' I turn to Kesia. 'What about if I told you that I can see the workhouse *and* a boy—'

Jacob clears his throat.

'All right. A *young man* called Jacob who lives in the workhouse. What if I told you that I could see *and* hear him?'

'Before, I would've said you were losing the plot, but . . . this is how you've got those letters, isn't it? He's your "special source"! And that original newspaper clipping you had. You've got them from the past!'

'I know it sounds crazy, but it's true,' I say. 'That mystery man I'm looking for is Jacob's dad. Jacob is the boy I see.' I turn back to him. 'Did you get my last letter? What does your dad look like?'

'*My father has a thick moustache, a beauty spot behind his ear and low cut here. I have a brooch that my mother gave me. It has a portrait of my father.*' Jacob takes off his flat cap and removes a delicate white handkerchief embroidered with his initials, J.E.A., with the brooch hidden inside. '*An old trick Felix showed me. My father bought the handkerchief for me. We have matching ones. I'll leave the brooch in the fireplace but please take good care of it; it's the only portrait I have of him.*'

'I will. We're so close to finding him. And there's something else—'

'Hold on,' Kesia whispers, and I know she's connected the dots. 'Wait, Isaiah, you can't tell him. You *can't* tell him about the fire—'

'What?' I whisper back but before I can say any more, Jacob continues.

'I've planned what I want to do about Mr Moore and this workhouse. We're protesting. It's only a few of us so far. I have organised our first meeting after lights out today.' Jacob balls the handkerchief in his hands. *'If we get enough people, Mr Moore will have to take notice!'*

'Be careful.'

'Yes, yes. What about your housing situation?'

'I will . . . uh . . . tell you about that later.'

'I need to go before Mr Moore sees me not doing my work. Farewell, friend.'

'Laters.'

Jacob is gone, leaving the special brooch with his dad's portrait in the fireplace. I pick it up and brush off the ash. It has a gold frame with gold and silver twisting wire surrounding a small oval painting of Jacob's dad. It looks like it was made by a professional.

Jacob and his father have the same wider nose and high forehead as me, but his dad has darker brown skin like mine.

'Whoa,' Kesia whispers, touching the edges of the brooch. 'This is . . . Whoa.'

'I know. I can't believe it either but it's true. Anyways, my dad says "can't" is not in our vocabulary.'

Kesia smashes her lips together, exhaling. 'My mum says that too.'

Leaving the basement, I plan with Kesia that we'll meet at the library at the weekend to investigate. I'd never tell her, but it feels good to have someone else knowing this secret. It feels too big to carry all by myself.

Dad: will be home late again
have an urgent appointment with Citizens Advice
we can do our Sunday together

'Isaiah, you're a busy guy,' Darius says from outside Clarice's door. 'Did you get my message?'

'Yeah, and I made a list.'

POSSIBLE CUSTOMERS OF MATTHEW & SONS

Ms Addams	Mr Johnson
Mr Whitaker	Miss Wright
Mr Zulu	Ms Davis
Ms Reddy	Mrs Stephens

Frowning, Darius looks down at the list. 'Are you sure this isn't too much? You have school.'

'No, I can do it.' *I can do it for Dad and me.*

'If you think it's fine, then we can make it work. Oh, yeah. Did you speak to your mum?'

'Yeah.'

'And?' Darius gestures with his hands. 'What did she say?'

'She was uh . . .'

Clarice pulls open her front door in old blue overalls this time. 'Are you both going to ever come inside? G.M. is hungry.'

She dumps the rabbit in my hands like a baby, along with a damp piece of lettuce that's larger than his whole body. 'You can make it up to him by feeding him.'

I stick the lettuce in front of G.M.'s mouth and he destroys it, almost nibbling half in a few seconds.

'You never said what I'm doing,' I say, following Clarice inside her flat. 'What am I fixing?'

Clarice holds up paintbrushes, shaking them. 'We're painting furniture.'

'But aren't you a painter? That's *your* job. Why would you need help with that?'

'Ah, because . . . I have a chair that I need help painting and . . . um . . . could be other furniture too.'

Darius says, 'Business is business, right, Isaiah? Your website says that you can do anything.'

He's right, but it doesn't make sense. Why would Clarice want me to help her paint a chair?

'All riiiiiight. Call me Picasso.'

'Fantastic, follow me,' Clarice says, and we pass the wooden easel I recognise that Dad's been working on.

'Did my dad make that for you?' I ask.

Her cheeks rise from all the smiling. 'Yes, isn't it wonderful? He was telling me about his woodworking. What a talented family.'

When did Dad have time to do this?

'Let's paint some chairs before you have to go home.'

Chapter Thirty-Three

Thursday

'What are you doing at the weekend?' Fredrick asks me during IT. 'We can go into town or the arcade again.'

I don't have money for that and neither does Dad. All the business money is going to rent, even if I have to make the landlord accept it.

I click through my website, pleased with the new photographs I've added. 'I'm going out with my dad on Sunday and working with Kesia on our history project on Saturday.'

'Spending the whole Saturday with your bestie, are you?

I ignore his teasing.

'I can come over to Kieran's on Saturday evening,' I say. 'We can play *FIFA* and I'll beat you. Again.'

'We'll see about that,' Fredrick replies. 'Do you wanna make a bet?'

I stare at him with a small grin on my face. I'm not stupid enough to ever bet my hard-earned money but he doesn't know that. 'When I take your money, don't cry.'

'You're the one who's gonna be crying,' Fredrick replies.

Mr Iyer walks towards our row, ending our conversation. 'Boys, please show me your websites so I can see your progress.' *Sniff.* 'I want to see how much you've been listening in our lessons.'

We bring up our websites, clicking our way through for Mr Iyer to see.

'Isaiah, this is very good.'

'I used a sans serif font because it makes it more accessible to my customers and it gives it a . . .' I pause, trying to remember what Mr Lim said. 'Clean finish.'

'Yes, excellent.'

'Fredrick leans over to look at my website. 'Help me with mine then. How did you get yours to look like that?'

I shrug. 'I'm talented.'

'Yeah, yeah. Whatever. Just help me with my website.'

When we're in history after IT, Mr Paterson says, 'As you all know, because I've been talking about it all term, our class trip to the Victorian exhibition is next week Thursday. Don't all cheer at once.'

A few students cheer and whoop, but I get a bitter taste in my mouth. The fire and the exhibition are on the same date. I don't feel ready and I'm running out of time. If

Mr Moore locks the dormitories at night, how will Jacob escape from the fire? How will he survive?

'Save that pitiful excuse of a cheer for someone else,' Mr Paterson comments. 'The purpose of the trip is a full immersion in the Victorian era, kindly funded by the school. In today's lesson, we're going to consider what it means to exhibit. First things first, hands up if you've ever visited an exhibition or museum.'

Hands fly up into the air around the room, including mine. When my parents were still together, we used to go all the time. The Faraday Museum is one of my favourites.

'That's what I like to see,' Mr Paterson says. 'Let's look at these pictures of The Great Exhibition of 1851. What do you think the Victorians were trying to say about themselves . . .'

Mr Paterson lobs newspapers and magazines on different tables. 'I want you all to get creative. If we were designing an exhibition about Britain today, what might we choose to display and how might we display it? I want you to create a poster. Choose any partner you want or work in groups. I'm feeling generous.'

The class comes alive as people grab the best magazines, stealing newspapers and glues to stick clippings down.

'I'm gonna cut out this article about that man who won

the world record for eating the most digestives,' Fredrick says, reading one of the magazines. 'What's more British than a digestive biscuit?'

'Custard creams! Those are my favourite. What else should go on it, Isaiah?' Kieran asks.

If I was telling them the truth, it would display bad landlords, poor treatment of people with disabilities and people going hungry. But I can't say any of that to my friends because they don't know what's going on, so I just shrug like I don't have an answer for once.

We work on our poster for the rest of the lesson. 'Well done, everyone,' Mr Paterson says. 'Final thing. You will have work to do during the trip next week.'

'*Nooo.*'

'*Why do we have to do work on a trip, sir? I thought it was going to be fun.*'

'Sorry to burst your bubble,' he replies. 'You're going to work your way through the exhibition, paying attention to the display labels and the information they give about the things displayed. What kind of story do they tell? That is all. Please pack away.'

While Mr Paterson talks to me and Kesia at the front, Kieran and Fredrick wait at the back, messing with the displays.

'Sooo. Tell me how ready you are,' he says to us. 'Do

you need help with anything? Do you want to do a run-through with me?'

'Yes, sir.' Kesia steps in before I can say anything. 'We just have some little things to add.'

'We'll be ready,' I add, forgetting about all the parts I still have left to do. And no time to do them in.

Chapter Thirty-Four

Saturday

'Have you worked on your personal response bit yet?' Kesia asks, watching out for the library phone to be free again.

'No, not yet,' I reply, distracted.

I'm not going to say anything personal.

Kesia's face looks pained. 'Why not? We have less than a week left now *and* we still need to finish off the last-minute interviews with your uncle, our headteacher and Reggie. Do you not want to win any more?'

'Why are you worrying so much?' I ask. 'We're going to win. I'll get it done.'

Kesia puts down her pen. 'Why are you always so busy? I know you don't wanna talk about it.'

'It's not like I wanna be busy all the time, but . . . because of my dad and his . . . ermm . . . pain, I look after him sometimes and do other things to make money.'

Kesia nods. 'I get it. When my mum lost her job and

my dad's hours got cut, I washed cars and walked people's dogs for extra money because I wanted to help, but my parents made me stop when they found out.'

What?

'Really?'

'Yeah. It's why I volunteer at the food bank. I like to give back and it keeps me busy – my parents work from home a lot. We didn't always have enough.'

Maybe there will be a time when we *do* all have enough.

Kesia picks her pen back up. 'I wanted to talk to you about Jacob and the fire.'

'What about it?'

'Do you think you should be trying to change the past?' she asks, putting her pen back down. 'The past can affect the present and future, Isaiah.'

Doesn't she get it? If we don't save Jacob, then he'll never reconnect with his dad. He'll miss out on that forever.

'I know you don't wanna hear it, but it's all connected – everything that has happened already, what's happening now and the things that come next. Don't try to stop the fire.'

'The phone is free.' I dart through the bookshelves, reaching the glass cubicle before anyone else can slip inside.

Kesia doesn't bring the fire up again.

We try the final hospital on our list, hoping that it's the one. Royal Oak. I can hear the woman on the phone clicking her mouse.

'Forties. Black man. A gold tooth at the back. A birthmark.'

'Yes,' Kesia and I say at the same time.

'The Royal Oak Hospital *did* have a patient with broken bones, fever and a skin rash as you described around that time, but he was discharged after two weeks. He was moved to a private specialist hospital.'

What?

'Why would he have been moved?' I ask.

'I have no information on that,' she replies. 'Is there anything else you need?'

'No.'

The phone goes dead.

I thought this would be it. I thought we'd find him for sure.

'He could be *anywhere*,' I say. Kesia taps her chin in thought. 'What is it?'

'People only get moved to specialist hospitals because those hospitals *specialise* in certain diseases or infections. But shouldn't we be focusing on figuring out what caused the fire?'

'Yeah, you're right. We should see what we can find about why it happened.'

We search, but there's nothing on what exactly caused

the fire. I bet Mr Moore buried it somewhere. I bet the fire must have something to do with him.

'Has Jacob told you anything about conditions in the workhouse? It could give us a clue and we could *guess* what could've caused it.'

'He's told me how terrible it was.' I have what they call a 'lightbulb' moment when something comes into my head. 'Oh, Jacob did get in trouble with Mr Moore for complaining about the insanitary and dangerous conditions. I can ask him more about it.'

'We can work with that.' Kesia's eyes gleam in response. *Ding. Ding. Ding.*

And as if the clock tower has overheard our conversation, I hear its ghostly chimes.

'Do you want to come see if he's in the basement?'

Kesia smiles. 'I wouldn't miss it for anything. Maybe I'll get to see him this time too!'

'I've got some news on your dad,' I say to Jacob through the shimmering, strange-coloured fire.

Jacob stares through the fireplace without his broom. *'Have you found him? Where is he?'*

I repeat what the woman on the phone told me. 'We think it's him. He matches your description.'

Jacob perks up. *'My father's close. I can feel it.'*

'Where's your broom?'

'We're refusing to work in protest of the conditions and Mr Moore's poor treatment. Word is spreading. I'm planning a huge protest in five days' time with some others. I wish you could see this, friend!'

Kesia prompts me. 'Ask him about the conditions.'

'Jacob, what makes the conditions at Cricklewood so bad?'

'Where do I begin? We sleep in cramped, insanitary conditions, sharing cheap wooden cots that were built for babies. Think about our postures!'

He's not giving me anything I can use. 'Anything else that looks like it's a hazard?'

'Anything else? The privies that they call toilets are disgusting and the food—'

Annoyed, I blurt out without thinking, 'But nothing that could cause a fire?'

The picture of people running out of the burning workhouse appears in my head.

'Is something the matter? What fire?'

Kesia kicks me hard in the ankle. She's glaring at me and shaking her head furiously.

Can I not even *tell* him about the fire? The fire that hasn't happened yet. How can I save him if I can't even warn him about it?!

'It's nothing.'

Chapter Thirty-Five

I close the basement door behind us.

'What is it, Isaiah?' Kesia asks, seeing my face.

'Why did you stop me in there?! It's like you don't want me to save him.'

She sighs. 'You wanted to warn Jacob about the fire! I said it before . . . don't meddle. What will happen will happen.'

I pace. 'But it's not right! How can I *not* tell my friend about the fire?' Because that's what Jacob is. My friend. 'I never found Jacob's death date and Mr Moore likes to lock them in the dormitory at night. Do you know what that means? Do you?'

'Of course I do.' Kesia lets out a hard sigh. 'But you can't try and change the past, Isaiah. You just *can't.*'

Ping.

Fredrick: where r u

hello

r u scared

'Who's that?'

'Just Fredrick. I kinda promised my friends that I'd go over to Kieran's house so we can play *FIFA*.'

'Oh, OK. Cool,' she says, kicking a piece of rubbish by the bins. 'I'll . . . see you at school then.'

'All right.' She doesn't move. 'Aren't you gonna go home?'

'My parents—'

'Work from home,' I finish off her sentence, remembering what she told me in the library.

'Yup.' Kesia pops the 'p'.

I know what it's like hanging around libraries or other places because you can't go home.

'Do you . . . uh . . . wanna come with me to Kieran's? I know you don't really talk to them, but they're cool. It's all right if you don't wanna.'

She shrugs. 'Yeah, I don't mind. It beats going back to the library.'

When we get to Kieran's house, his dad answers the door, leading us in. '*Isaiah, hoe gaat het met je?* Kieran said you were stopping by.'

Kieran's dad reminds me of a storm with his grey hair,

eyes and beard, and imposing build. 'Hi, Mr Alders, I'm all right. When did you get back?'

'Last night.' The storm blows Kesia's way. 'Who are you?'

Mr Alders is very blunt and straight to the point.

'Hi, I'm Kesia. I go to school with Kieran, Isaiah and Fredrick.'

'Ah, schoolmates. Come in.'

When Mr Alders' back is turned, Kesia mouths, *OMG.*

Her eyes take in Kieran's house. It's huge and the complete opposite of our flats, but it's so modern and new it feels like it has no story behind it. Kind of massive but boring.

Fredrick and Kieran come down the stairs. They slow down once they see Kesia standing beside me.

'What's *she* doing here?' Fredrick asks, pointing to Kesia.

Kieran slaps Fredrick in the arm. 'Hi, Kesia.'

She waves back. 'Hey, Kieran.'

Kieran's dad has his arm around Kieran's mum's waist. They watch our interaction.

'Hi, Isaiah and Kesia, is it?' Kieran's mum asks, smiling at her. 'Is this one of your new friends, Kieran?'

'Kesia is my friend,' I reply, my face heating up a bit. 'But she's in the same class as all of us. Kesia's doing the Victorian exhibition project with me.'

'Kesia, you must be as smart as our Isaiah then.' Kieran's mum beams.

Kesia leans in with a reply. 'I'm smarter.'

'Ooooh,' Fredrick teases, and Kieran's dad's laughter booms like it's on loudspeaker.

'Only in history,' I say back. 'You all know I'm the smartest at *everything* else.'

'*Je l'aime bien*,' Kieran's mum whispers to Kieran's dad. 'It's nice to meet you, Kesia. I'm cooking fish tonight and there's plenty. Please say you'll stay for that.'

A smile grows like weeds on Kesia's face. 'All right, thank you.'

While we're waiting for dinner, Fredrick chucks me a controller to play *FIFA*. 'Time for me to beat you.'

'Why don't we show them our presentation first?' Kesia comments.

'Just say that you don't know how to play the game if that's what you mean,' Fredrick remarks, and Kesia snatches the controller off him.

'I don't, but I bet I can still beat you.'

And she does. Badly. Kieran and I film it for evidence.

'Whatever, man,' Fredrick sulks. 'I wasn't even playing my best. It doesn't count!'

'Yes, it does.' Kieran laughs, slapping his leg. 'Let's hear your presentation then.'

Using Kieran's laptop, we get up our presentation and Kesia starts off. 'Good afternoon, everyone. We're going to be looking at our connection with the past through letters, a map and interviews . . .'

'. . . that's it,' I finish. 'What do you think?'

Fredrick claps loudly like he's at an awards show.

'It's good. And what about this mystery man?' Kieran asks. 'Did you ever find him? Did Jacob ever reunite with his dad?'

'Yeah. We're almost there,' I reply, rocks settling at the bottom of my stomach as all I can think about is the workhouse fire.

'I love mysteries.' Kieran hands Kesia a controller. 'Let's play another game so I can watch Fredrick cry a second time.' Kieran teases him.

'I didn't cry!' Fredrick yells and then starts laughing. 'I swear! My eyes were dry.'

Chapter Thirty-Six

Sunday

'Wake up.' Dad's fully dressed and blurry figure hangs over me, shaking my shoulder gently. 'Isaiah, wake up.'

'Dad.' I groan, rubbing the sleep out of my eyes. 'What time is it? Why are you dressed?'

'It's early. Get ready and meet in the living room in fifteen minutes,' he replies.

Dad and I usually lie in on Sundays. When I get up, I cook whatever food we have left in the flat for breakfast. It's our 'Sunday jumble'.

'Hurry up, young blood!' Uncle Kwame shouts from somewhere in the flat.

I jump out of bed, forgetting that I was ever tired. 'Are we going somewhere?'

'Yes.' Dad laughs. 'No more questions. Go and get ready.'

I'm done with showering in record time. I throw on the last clean clothes I have left, hurrying to the living room with my jumper half on. Dad and Uncle Kwame are drinking instant coffee.

'I don't know how you can stomach this stuff.' Uncle Kwame's face pinches like he's sucked a lemon. 'Young blood, you're ready. You're going to need a coat and your whiteboard.'

'You're really not gonna tell me where we're going?' I ask, putting on my coat like Uncle Kwame said.

'Nope.'

'Oh yeah. I need to interview you later for my history exhibition project.'

'Anything for you, young blood. When you make it big, I'm going to claim some of the glory.'

We leave the flat, turning into side streets that I've never taken before. We pause outside a red-brick building with iron railings and gates. The Floyd Foyle Institute. There is a Black man waiting outside the building, who breaks out into rap. '*This here is the old Shepten, sharing history so we can live again.*'

Uncle Kwame and Dad roar with laughter at this.

'Martin, you *still* can't rap,' Uncle Kwame says, wiping tears from his eyes. 'I don't know why you won't give it up. We came here for a private tour of Shepten, not a concert.'

Martin opens his mouth to say something but stops with

a frown on his face. 'Fine. We can do the tour *without* any audio entertainment.' He sticks his hand out for me to shake. 'I'm Martin. I'm old friends with your father and Uncle Kwame. I work as Heritage Manager for the Shepten council. I oversee the teams who take care of buildings, monuments and places valued for their cultural and historical importance.'

'What's better than having a personal tour from someone who knows the history of Shepten inside and out?' Dad explains. 'Did I do good, son?'

My head bobs up and down as I nod. 'Yeah, we're gonna win with this!'

Dad ruffles my hair and Uncle Kwame claps his palm with mine. 'That's what I like to hear.'

'Can we take short breaks for my dad?' I ask Martin, thinking about him walking for long without stopping.

Dad's face stretches into a smile. 'Always looking out for me, but I should be OK.'

'Yes, of course. We can take breaks and since your father and uncle won't let me rap, I'll just tell you the history instead,' Martin says, pointing to the building behind us. 'Shepten was once known as a working-class area with factories, workhouses and warehouses. It was in this area that Dr Floyd Foyle was born in 1708 to a working-class family. He always wanted more . . . *dreamt* of more and it was here in his parents' basement that young Floyd made a scientific discovery that would change medicine forever. He decided, once he was older, to convert his parents' house into an institute of science, providing scholarships for other working-class students who wanted to pursue science but couldn't afford it.'

I scribble down notes on my whiteboard.

'It's why my middle name is Floyd,' Uncle Kwame says, and chuckles a little. 'My dad thought some of the smartness would rub off on me through the name, but it didn't work out that way.'

Dad clasps Uncle Kwame's shoulder. 'You were the first one in our whole group to start and run their own successful business. You're opening up your second barbershop soon too.'

He punches Dad softly in his arm. 'Brother, *you* were the first to start and run their own successful business.'

Dad smiles, staring into the distance before he says, 'Let's move on to the next stop on the tour, Martin.'

The next stop is Shepten Swimming Pool. I've been here a couple times with my friends because we can swim for free.

'In 1846, the Baths and Washhouses Act was passed to encourage local authorities to build public baths and washhouses,' Martin says. 'Your dad and uncle could use a visit here.' He holds his nose.

Uncle Kwame burst out laughing. 'You're being childish.'

'That's what you get for not letting me rap!' Martin shouts, laughing. 'Isaiah, this is now a tour of how much I hate your dad and uncle's guts.'

'I'm going to report you,' Dad jokes, stroking his back.

'What's next, Martin?' I ask, noticing Dad's pain.

'Oh, right. There were separate entrances for men and women as you can see.' Martin points to the engravings at the entrance of the swimming pool. 'On to the next stop.'

The whole tour lasts around an hour and we visit places that I never knew existed like the Shepten Stadium and the Shepten Boys' Club.

Uncle Kwame treats us to a big breakfast at the local café after the tour. 'Young blood, pass me the ketchup for my eggs.'

Me: I have a secret weapon for our presentation

Kesia: what is it?

Isaiah

Tell me

I pass the ketchup.

'I hope you can see how great our home town is,' Dad says to me. 'Be proud of where you live.'

Chapter Thirty-Seven

Monday

'We're starting the process of evaluation for your websites, which is a crucial part of the process,' Mr Iyer says. He uncaps the board marker and writes: 'peer evaluation' and 'self-evaluation'.

I slide over my phone to Kesia with all the notes from our tour with Martin and everything I've learnt from Jacob. As she skims through, she bounces in her seat, a wide grin forming across her face.

'Who knows the difference between "peer evaluation" and "self-evaluation"? Isaiah?'

'Peer evaluation means that someone else evaluates, like a partner or something, and self-evaluation is when you evaluate your work by yourself,' I respond.

'Yes, that's correct.'

'We need to add all of this to our presentation,' she whispers. 'The map only has half of this so far . . . We're so gonna win!'

I laugh. 'That's what *I* said. Keep reading. I did the interview with my uncle.'

Interview with Uncle Kwame (owner of barbershop) – Transcript

Isaiah: 'Did you know that your barbershop used to be a Victorian convenience store called William Webster?'

Uncle K: 'I heard something about the history before I bought it, but I don't know much about the store. What did they sell?'

Isaiah: 'So many things. Teas, sugars, cocoa, spices, preserves, bees wax, black lead, putty powder, lamp black, linseed, brimstone, bloater paste, potted ham, semolina.'

Uncle K: 'Ha. I don't know what half of that stuff is, but that's great. It sounds like the store was necessary – the same for the barbershop because no one wants to be rolling around with scruffy hair . . .'

'Nice,' Kesia says. 'I have the interview with Reggie and our headteacher, Mr Rowan, soon too.'

'Turning to the person sitting next to you, I want you to start evaluating their website,' Mr Iyer says. 'You will pick out the good points and any areas in which they could do better. Get started.'

I partner with Kieran, and Fredrick finds someone else to go with.

Kieran shows me his trainer-customising website with his own artwork on the front page and different customised trainers.

'Your website is great,' I say, praising him. 'I'm giving you full marks – no areas for improvement.'

'Thanks.' Kieran's fist bumps mine. 'Look what I added.' He plays the video on the main homepage. It's him, Fredrick and other people from the class modelling different customised trainers.

I play the video again. 'When did you do all this?' I ask. 'And why didn't you ask me to be in it?!'

Others from the class turn, crowding around Kieran's computer to watch the trailer. He even used one of Darius's songs for the background music.

'I didn't ask you cos you're always busy,' Kieran confesses. 'But I did want you to be in it.'

My phone pings.

Dad: a package came for you
picture of a drone

'Yes,' I whisper.

I knew Mum wouldn't let me down.

'What?' Kieran asks, and I show him the picture of the drone. 'Drooooonnnne! I'm coming to yours after school, man.'

'I'm coming too,' Fredrick butts in from across the room. 'I wanna play with that drone.'

At lunchtime, Kesia and I are tucked in the corner of the school's library working on the computers. I'm scrolling through pages of archives, searching for anything on the Cricklewood Workhouse fire.

'I found the inquest,' I say, a spark of hope unfurling in my stomach.

An inquest opened by deputy coroner, Mr P. DAVIS, and Mr C. VANCLEAVES, warden of Cricklewood Workhouse.

Mr MOORE the workhouse guardian stated that two days before the fire, he began evacuating all the children from the workhouse for safety concerns over the fireplaces. He noticed more black soot in and around the fireplaces and very dark smoke coming from the chimneys, particularly from the fireplace in the boys' basement dormitory.

Our fireplace.

He had planned an inspection of the fireplaces the day before the fire. Mr Moore believes some children may have gone back inside the workhouse to collect their belongings. Witnesses were unable to confirm this.

The cause of the fire was said to be a combination of a build-up of tar in the chimney flutes, which is highly combustible when ignited, and loose bed clothing getting caught by a candle flame.

'I don't trust Mr Moore, but if the basement fireplace in our flats was one of the things that caused the fire, then I'll clean it,' I say. 'I have to stop the fire.'

'But, Isaiah, you're cleaning it in the present not the past! It might not change anything, however much you want it to. Sometimes you have to accept the past for what it is. Isaiah, you do know that.'

'No, I don't! Why do you wanna give up instead of trying? You want Jacob to die!'

Kesia's eyes fill with tears and she storms out of the library.

I'll just do this on my own then. Like always.

Me: can we cancel the appointment
for after school today?

Darius: yeah, sure. Everything OK?

Me: Yeah. Something important I have to do.

Chapter Thirty-Eight

I borrow what I can and then use some of my business money to buy cloths, masks, flashlights, brushes, rods, creosote remover and protective glasses to clean the fireplace. It's not enough, but it's the best I could get. There's no note in the fireplace from Jacob. I hope he's all right.

Balancing my phone on my seat in the basement, I watch an instructional video on how to clean a fireplace.

The basement door creaks. 'I hope you didn't start without me,' Kesia says, fiddling with the zip on an old bobbly tracksuit.

'What are you doing here?' I ask.

'You didn't really think I was gonna let you do this by yourself, did you?'

I clear my throat. 'Thanks. And . . . I didn't mean what I said earlier, about you giving up and not trying or about wanting Jacob to die. Sorry. I know you don't. I think you try harder than anyone else I know.'

She smiles. 'I'm not sure how much help I'm gonna be because I can't clean out the fireplace. The ash could trigger a chest crisis.'

'Oh, here you go.' I quickly grab a mask and Kesia secures it around her face. 'You can instruct me on what to do from the video.'

'Deal. The video says you should remove the ash from it first . . .'

By the time we're done, I'm covered in dirt *and* ash, so I keep away from Kesia, but I'm not sure cleaning it was enough. 'We'll know tomorrow if it's worked.'

'I'll see you tomorrow, Isaiah. Mr Paterson said we can run through our presentations with him.'

When I get into the flat, there's a box waiting by the door. I drop to my knees, ripping it open to see my drone. It's not the DR4X, but I don't care.

I video-call Mum.

'I'm guessing you saw your gift. I know it's not the exact one you asked for, but the tech department at my university gave me a discount,' Mum says with a teasing smile. *'Why are you covered in dirt?'*

'Thanks, Mum, I love it! And . . . I was helping a friend clean a fireplace.'

'You're welcome, and don't they have professionals to do that?'

'Mum, I have to go! My friends are coming over. Bye!'

'OK, I'll speak to you soon.'

I run to the bathroom, stripping off my filthy clothes on the way. The cold water hits my body but I can't use any extra hot water because then we won't have any tomorrow. As I'm shrugging on my hoodie, the doorbell goes. 'I'm coming!'

When I open the door, Fredrick pushes past me and asks, 'Where's the drone?'

'Not even a "hello" or nothing.' I laugh. 'It's in my room.'

Kieran closes the door behind him. 'I haven't been to your house in ages.'

'There's not much to do here – your house is better.'

When we get to my room, Fredrick has already taken the drone out of the box and is flying it around with the remote control. 'This is cool.'

'Darius was saying you've been going to a lot of houses,' Kieran remarks.

'Yeah.' I take out the stash of money from under my mattress, adding in the change from the supplies I bought today. 'Look at it!'

Laughing, I wave the money about as Fredrick attempts

to grab some. When I see Dad frowning in the doorway, I stop.

'Where did you get that money from?' he asks.

I hide the money behind my back. 'I . . . erm . . . it's for my IT project. You know, the one I was telling you about. We had to set up a business and I decided on a handyman business. I fixed people's things for money.'

'And your school just allowed you to do this,' Dad says, moving closer to me. 'Your school endorsed you going into strangers' houses alone—'

'He went with my cousin Darius, not on his own.' Kieran backs me up.

'And none of them were proper strangers. It was people from the building and Uncle Kwame.'

'What did you need the money for, Isaiah?' He asks the question I don't want him to ask. His voice is getting louder and quieter both at the same time. Deadly. 'Did you want to show off to your friends?'

My face is burning up. Why is this happening in front of them? Why are my friends *still* here?

'Because why else would my son, *who I told to focus on school*, be sneaking around to other people's houses! What is the money for?'

'It was for us, OK,' I choke out after a while. 'I didn't want the landlord to take away our home.'

The anger drains from Dad's face as my words hit him. 'Boys, I think it's time you went home.'

Kieran hastily puts the drone back inside the box and shoves Fredrick out of the room. 'Bye, Isaiah.'

I can't look at them.

When the front door slams, Dad says, 'I was finding a way. Citizens Advice said we have grounds to fight back; discrimination they said. I told you to trust me. I'm not going to allow anything to happen to you, Isaiah. It's just you and me.'

'And Mum.'

'She's not here.'

'I just wanted to help,' I plead. 'I wanted to make sure that it wouldn't happen.'

Someone knocks at the door. 'Maybe one of my friends forgot something.'

Dad goes to answer it with me following behind. But it's not my friends, it's our landlord.

'Mr Oni. Is this how you're going to play the game?' he asks. 'You sent your son to go around with his fake business to start fixing "problems" in the other flats I own? He's stirring up trouble.'

Dad moves me behind him as a barrier, but I sneak under his arm. 'I didn't *send* my son to do anything and if it was broken, he was fixing things that needed to be fixed.'

'You just wanna kick us out on the street.'

'I came to tell you to stop whatever it is you're doing,' he replies. 'I'll be happy to see the back of you.'

I take the money out of my pocket and shove it at him. 'Take your money, that's all you care about.'

The landlord counts then pockets the money. 'It's something, but it's not enough and it's *far* too late.'

'We will see about that.' Dad slams the door in his face and hobbles over to the sofa, his breathing heavy. 'You should go to bed.'

'Do you want me to get the hot-water bottle for you?'

'Go to bed, Isaiah!' he shouts. 'You have school in the morning, and I don't want you to be late. We don't need extra attention on us.'

'But—'

'No,' Dad breathes. 'Bed. Now. You don't *need* to do anything, Isaiah. I'm tired. I'm tired of it all.'

I go to bed, but I can't sleep.

What are we going to do?

Chapter Thirty-Nine

Tuesday

'Arghhhhh.'

'Dad?' I speak, my voice groggy.

'Arghhhhh!'

Thump.

'Dad!' I shout, stumbling to the living room. Dad is in pain on the floor. It looks unbearable, etched deep into his face. He doesn't even open his eyes to look up at me.

'I . . . can't . . . move.' He struggles to get the words out from between his teeth. 'Hospital.'

I scramble for Dad's phone to call an ambulance. There's a message from mum.

Mum: We need to talk.
Please answer your phone.

I swipe it away and call the ambulance for Dad. We

wait for what feels like hours until it shows up and then I go with him.

Hours later, I help Dad on to the sofa bed, making sure there are enough pillows supporting his back.

'Is that enough?' I ask, adjusting the pillows. 'Do you need more?'

'Yes, it's fine, Isaiah,' Dad replies, gesturing for the strong medication the doctor prescribed him. 'Can you get me some water, please?'

'OK.'

I turn on the tap. The water sloshes over my hand as it fills the chipped mug. I set the mug on the table and turn on the TV, sitting down beside him. Dad's phone is still in my pocket. I take it out and see part of an email from my school on the screen, but I don't unlock it.

Dear Mr Oni,

   We have logged Isaiah's unexplained absence today. Please can you contact the school to discuss further.

There are many missed calls from Mum and angry texts. I can imagine her rubbing her forehead in frustration.

When my phone rings, Dad has dozed off, hugging the hot-water bottle.

'Hi, Mum,' I whisper.

'Isaiah, oh, thank God! I've been calling your dad. What happened? Why didn't you go to school?'

'It was Dad. We had to go to the hospital.'

'Oh no, how is he?'

'Better now, but I have something to tell you,' I whisper, the sofa vibrating from Dad's snores.

'Did something happen?'

I can't keep it from her any longer. 'We're . . . uh . . . having some trouble with the landlord. It's more than the late rent payments—'

Mum sighs. *'What late rent payments? Your father didn't say anything about being late on his rent. Is he there?'*

'He's sleeping. And don't blame him, Mum. He doesn't like to bother you.'

Dad's the one who's always here for me.

'If it concerns you, Isaiah, he wouldn't be bothering me. I will call back once he's awake and see what I can do to help. I'll speak to you soon. Bye.'

I check the messages on my phone.

Kieran: y didn't you come skl

Fredrick: u bunking again

I wonder if they've told anyone yet about Dad and me being evicted. I wonder if the whole school already knows. I ignore their messages.

Kesia: Hi
You weren't in school. Are you OK? Was it your dad?

                   Me: yeah, but he's all right. And some other stuff

Kesia: is it to do with the landlord? I heard him shouting outside your door. I didn't mean to snoop

Kesia knows now too.

Kesia: I won't tell anyone.
He's horrible to my parents too.
have you checked the basement yet

How could I forget? I need to go there now!

                   Me: Are you home? Meet you down there

Did it work? Did I stop the fire? Is Jacob safe?

As I'm rushing down the stairs to the basement, I trip and my body slams against the wall. The space around me flickers, changing before my eyes. Opposite me, Jacob slams his body into a locked door.

'*I demand you to let me out, Mr Moore! Let me out this instant!*'

'Jacob!' The room disappears.

'Isaiah, what's wrong?' Kesia asks, coming up behind me.

'It's Jacob. Mr Moore locked him in a cupboard again!'

'If he's locked in, do you know what that means, Isaiah?'

My heart beats sluggishly. 'It means that Mr Moore *was* lying in the report. He didn't evacuate the workhouse.'

We run the rest of the way into the basement and I scribble a note for Jacob. I don't know if he'll see it before it's too late, but I have to try.

Jacob. I hope you see this note. There's going to be a fire at Cricklewood. I don't know how, but you need to get out. Send me a sign that you made it.

Isaiah

I throw the note into the fire and watch it burn.

Chapter Forty

Wednesday

Mr Paterson finishes off the lesson, but Fredrick has been talking for most of it, trying to find out where I was yesterday. Weirdly, he hasn't mentioned the fight I had with my dad . . . yet.

'Are you really not gonna tell us?' Fredrick asks.

Kieran watches me, waiting to see what I say. My stomach is like a wet towel being wrung after swimming.

'Is this because of the whole landlord eviction thing?' Fredrick asks. 'I swear we didn't tell anyone.'

'You didn't?'

'Why would we tell anyone about that?' Kieran asks, confused. 'We don't want you to move away. You're my best friend and you know how bad Fredrick is at *FIFA*.' Kieran teases him. 'I'm only playing. You're all right.'

'What's gonna happen now . . . with the landlord?' Fredrick asks.

'Dad's trying to get someone to stop it from happening.'

'All right,' Kieran replies.

'And my dad had to go hospital. That's why I wasn't at school.'

Fredrick's eyebrow wrinkles. 'Oh . . . uh, is he all right?'

'Yeah, he's better than he was . . .' Usually I wouldn't say anything else, but today it's important that I do. 'He has chronic pain, so the pain doesn't go away. Ever.'

My friends look stunned, like this isn't something that they've ever thought of being possible.

'That must be hard – for your dad, I mean,' Fredrick says. 'Being in pain all the time.'

'Seems like our time is up.' Mr Paterson pouts, but we can tell he's faking. 'I will now cry into my freshly baked oatmeal raisin cookies my mum made for me.'

'You're like, fifty, sir. Do you still live with your mum?'

'I'll have you know that I'm actually a hundred and five years old and I'm waiting for my mum to die so I can live off her insurance money.'

A gasp.

'That's evil, sir.'

'It was a joke. Ha ha. Don't tell your parents,' Mr Paterson adds. 'Please don't forget to bring your packed lunches tomorrow.' Once everyone leaves the classroom, he faces Kesia and I. 'OK, dream team. I'm ready to hear what you have.'

Kesia unfolds out the largest sheet of paper I've ever seen, with our makeshift map printed on it. Where did she print that off?

'Nancy,' she answers my unsaid question. 'This is our map of Shepten.'

'We'll show what things were before and what they are now,' I continue. 'It was Kesia's idea to do short interviews with the people in these places, like my uncle Kwame who owns the barbershop, which used to be the convenience store, William Webster.'

Kesia gives me a thumbs up.

'Extra points for more research,' Mr Paterson says. 'I'm guessing you have other interviews too?'

'Yes of course,' Kesia butts in. She takes out the transcripts of her interviews and I scan Mr Rowan's interview.

Kesia: Thanks for speaking to me, Mr Rowan.

Mr Rowan: Thank you for doing a thorough job at representing our school.

Kesia: Did you know that the school used to be Shepten Hospital?

Mr Rowan: Yes, I was aware of its history.

When my wife came to visit the school, she said she could almost feel people from the past here. I don't believe in the supernatural and it was probably all in her imagination. Can you imagine people from the past lingering in the present?

Kesia: Yeah. Imagine. Do you think that this building once being a hospital deepens your connection to it?

Mr Rowan: Yes, in a way because a hospital is such an important place and Shepten Hospital was the exact place my great-great-grandfather was saved after contracting smallpox. Did you know this hospital was also a specialist centre?

Kesia: No, sir. For what?

Mr Rowan: For skin rashes and skin disease.

Could it be?

Didn't Jacob's dad have skin rashes? When Jacob first told me his story, he didn't say he travelled far to get to Cricklewood. Could Jacob's dad be in Shepten Hospital?

'Is it him?' I ask myself.

'Is who him?' Mr Paterson asks. 'Is this part of your

presentation for tomorrow? Because I love it. Mysterious.'

My chest pulses. 'It must be him.' *Ding. Ding. Ding.*

The history room falls away to reveal the grainy black-and-white hospital ward. The nurse greets her patient. 'Good day, sir.'

I crane my neck round to finally see the man's face.

He looks *exactly* like he does in his portrait.

Emmanuel Akintola.

He's been right under my nose this whole time.

Sitting up in his bed, Jacob's dad coughs into his white embroidered handkerchief, the initials E.O.A. are plain to see. 'Do I have no visitors today, as usual? Not one? Something has happened to my son. I know it.'

'Sorry, sir. No visitors for you still.'

The room changes back to the history room and Kesia stares at me, waiting for me to reply to Mr Paterson. But I can't. I've just seen Jacob's dad.

I run all the way home from school, not stopping once until I'm standing in front of the fireplace. It's empty. I throw something in and wait for the fire with trembling hands, but nothing happens. Jacob doesn't appear.

Jacob. I have some news for you about your dad.

When I get into the flat, I call for my dad and hear movement in the kitchen. 'How's your back?'

243

'A bit better, thanks,' he replies, hobbling into the living room with his bowl of chicken curry and rice. 'Your food is over there.'

'Thanks.' I settle down beside him on the sofa with the piping-hot bowl resting on my thigh, feeling the heat.

'Don't burn yourself, Isaiah. Put the bowl down on the table.' I do what he says. 'How was school?'

I tell him all about it, but I can see he's not really listening.

'Isaiah, do you want to go and live with your mum?' Dad asks out of nowhere. 'If you want to, I understand.'

I face him. 'Why would you think I'd wanna live with Mum?'

'Because clearly I haven't been doing a good enough job of raising you myself, especially this past year.' Dad breathes. 'And now your mother knows about the rent issues. Moving to Shepten was a mistake.'

'No, it wasn't. Shepten has been the best. I'm with Uncle Kwame and I have my friends and school and *you*.'

Dad doesn't say anything else. He just eats his rice and curry.

Chapter Forty-One

Thursday

I'm nervous. I'm *never* nervous. But today I'm super nervous. It's exhibition day and the same date as the great fire.

'Are you nervous?' Kesia asks as she skims her notes. 'I don't think I've ever seen you nervous before.'

I throw on my casual smile. 'Only a bit.'

Students from our school and other schools mill around the exhibition, while we set up on the stage at the front.

My phone vibrates with messages from people wishing me good luck.

Mum: you'll do amazing x

Uncle Kwame: you've got this, young blood

Dad: I know your name will be up there with the greats one day

Kieran's mum: Hi, Isaiah. It's Kieran's mum. Good luck with the presentation today. I know you'll represent the school well.

'Isaiah,' Kieran calls me. 'Are you ready?'

I nod. 'Yeah. Where's Fredrick?'

Kieran bursts out laughing. 'He's in trouble with one of the teachers because he tried to squeeze his foot into an old Victorian shoe after I dared him.'

I laugh because Fredrick never backs down from a dare.

The exhibition organiser gets on the stage. 'We're about to start. Please take your seats.'

Kieran punches me in the arm. 'Don't forget your words.'

The crowd eventually settles. I sit by Kesia right at the front with the rest of the students presenting.

'Welcome to all the schools,' the organiser says. 'We've had a fabulous time curating this exhibition at Shepten Museum. Today, we have several students ready to present on the theme – our connections with the past. Let's welcome our first set of students from the Maple Hills Secondary School.'

Everyone in the audience claps for Kesia and me as we get on the stage. We set up our presentation so it'll be projected on to the white screen behind.

'Hi, everyone. My name is Kesia and this is Isaiah and we're from Maple Hills. When we first heard what the theme was, we were excited to explore the history of Shepten.'

'Shepten has great links with the past,' I continue. 'We

studied some of its history in class with our teacher, Mr Paterson.'

Mr Paterson stands up and points to himself and bows, making everyone laugh.

'We came up with this map of Shepten and the history connected to these places,' Kesia says, changing the PowerPoint slide. 'While Charles Booth's "map of London" showed poverty in London, *our* map shows the connection Shepten has with its past. We interviewed the people who currently use those buildings . . .'

'I spoke to my uncle Kwame about his barbershop that used to be a convenience store called William Webster . . . different people have different connections to the past. The last one on our list was Cricklewood Workhouse, which is now the block of flats where Kesia and I both live.' I pull at the collar of my school shirt; it feels like it's strangling me. 'The Cricklewood workhouse was opened in 1727 until a fire destroyed it in 1838.'

The slide changes to the letters from Jacob. I'd retyped some of them, leaving out all the parts he didn't want included. 'Before I talk about the letters, I want to show you an original fountain pen from the nineteenth century.' I take out Jacob's golden pen, presenting it to the audience. 'Fountain pens were a big thing in the eighteen hundreds.

'These letters are between me and Jacob, a boy who

would've stayed in Cricklewood Workhouse. Jacob is thirteen like me and he was sent to live there after his dad went missing at sea. His dad wasn't just an entrepreneur or a merchant; he also helped enslaved people. The Slavery Abolition Act was passed in 1833, which meant that enslaved people were officially free in the British Empire, but slavery continued in places like the US, Cuba and Brazil. Jacob has a privileged life; his mum was from a noble family. Basically, they were *stinky* rich.' People laugh around the room. 'But Jacob wasn't that close to the rest of his mum's family and after she passed away from TB, it was just him and his dad.' *Until we met in the fireplace.* 'Jacob had to do all kinds of chores at Cricklewood like sweeping out the fireplaces, which is *really* hard, if you didn't know. I tried it – wouldn't recommend.' The crowd laughs again. 'I'd take washing the plates over that any day.'

There are mumblings from the crowd as people get into the 'story' I'm telling, not realising it is real.

'Jacob ended up getting a job at the convenience store, William Webster. This was after he tried to make money singing on the street. Did you know there were "prime" street corners to make money? You see . . . I feel more of a personal connection with the . . . uh . . . Jacob because of how similar our lives are . . .' I swallow. *Can I share this with everyone?* 'Like the boy from the letters, my dad and I ermm . . .' I can feel Kesia watching me. 'It's just him and me, like it's Jacob and his dad. And . . . ermm . . . in the workhouse Jacob didn't have any money and . . . ermm . . . neither do I.' *What am I saying?*

'Some human experiences are common across time. Especially the ones that shouldn't be.' I put down my notes. 'I wasn't gonna say this, but I'm trying to be honest. My friends don't even know the full story . . . no one does. Over a year ago, my dad had an accident at work. He messed up his back and now he can't work properly. He has chronic pain. He's in pain *all* of the time. Because he can't work, we can't . . . ermm . . . always afford things. I have to think of ways to get around that. Ways to help.' I swallow. 'It's easy for us to think of experiences in history as things that were only there in the past, like workhouses. But even though we're talking about a period in history nearly two hundred years ago, the poverty then is still normal now. I know that. I've lived that.' There's an intense silence in the room. 'So that's what I wanted to say. Kesia is going to talk about her connection now.'

I clear my throat and step back. It feels like everyone is staring at me.

Once we're done, we settle into our seats and wait for everyone else to present.

I can't believe I just did that.
I can't believe everyone knows.

'Thanks so much to all the pupils who presented today,' the organiser says. 'I'm going to discuss with the judges now and will be back with a decision soon. I say judges, but it's just me and the museum staff.' People laugh. 'Be back in a jiffy.'

'Well done, dream team!' Mr Paterson praises us. 'You did *extremely* well and that's big coming from me. Your personal connection touched everyone, Isaiah. I have never heard an audience so stilled.'

Kieran and Fredrick both grab a shoulder each, tousling me from side to side like a puck in a game of air hockey.

'Get off me, man,' I say, laughing.

The organiser returns to the stage with a huge cheque for £250. The audience quietens down, settling in their seats.

'We want to say a big thank you again to all the schools who participated today. We've decided to go with *this* school in particular because of the depth of connections they've explored and the resonance of their work. I think we can all say that they have brought history to life like no one else. So, without leaving you all waiting for too long, the winners are . . . Maple Hills with Kesia and Isaiah. Please come up on to the stage and collect your prize.'

Slaps rain down my back as we get up to collect the cheque. We actually did it! Kesia holds one end of it and I hold the other for a photograph. We won together. Mr Paterson manages to slip in to get a picture taken with us too.

'My dream team wins.' He pats himself on the back. 'Maybe I'm an amazing teacher after all.'

'You're all right, sir,' I joke.

'We did it,' Kesia whispers to me, smiling.

'Yeah, we did,' I smile back.

Ding. Ding. Ding.

The chiming bells of the clock tower don't stop this time.

Ding. Ding. Ding.

As I run down the street towards our block of flats, the colour around me changes into black and white, flickering as hundreds of people charge past me, disappearing into thin air.

'Jacob!' I shout, rushing past children with faces covered in soot, choking on the thick black smoke, eyes streaming with tears. 'Jacob!'

I run into the basement and hurl some paper into the fireplace. Through the strange flames I can see the boy's dormitory has been completely destroyed, with black walls and charred beds.

'Jacob? Jacob!'

I didn't stop the fire. I didn't save him . . .

Then I spot something white under the ashes and soot in the fireplace. I carefully lift it out and turn it over. It's a handkerchief. And neatly embroidered in the corner are the initials J.E.A.

Chapter Forty-Two

The next morning, I'm at school, and I should be celebrating our exhibition win, but I'm on edge.

'We're now going to begin the self-evaluation process,' Mr Iyer says. 'Take a look at your websites: What do you think you did well? What do you think you can improve on? What are your overall thoughts on the process?'

I used the right colours that were suitable for my audience.

Fredrick and Kieran are distracted, watching a parkour video instead of working on their evaluations.

'What happened?' Kesia whispers, sticking her head between the computer screens, so she looks like a hotdog.

I dig the handkerchief out of my pocket and show it to her. 'This.'

Kesia takes the handkerchief, stroking it. 'It's a sign! It *has* to be. His father gave that to him. It's one of the only things he kept!' Mr Iyer turns to look our way. Kesia ducks. 'What are you gonna do?'

'If he survived, he should be in Shepten Hospital somewhere. And that's here, this school! The inquest said all survivors were brought here,' I whisper. 'I'm going to look at lunch.'

'I can help you.'

I shake my head. 'Thanks, but I don't think you can see what I'm looking for. You only ever saw the dormitory through the fireplace.'

'All right, but I want to know *everything* that happens.'

I watch the clock for the rest of the lesson. Is time moving backwards?

'Why'd you keep on watching the time?' Kieran asks.

'I need to go and do something for a friend at lunch.' I hope he doesn't ask me any more questions. 'But I'll come and meet you guys by the field.'

'All right, but message me if you need any help. Which friend is—'

Bringggg!

Saved by the bell.

'Pack away. If you haven't finished your self-evaluation forms, finish them over the weekend and bring them back to class next lesson. No excuses. I'm looking forward to grading your websites.'

I hurry out of the classroom, heading towards the first floor of the building.

I push past students in the hallway, ducking when I see teachers. I look inside each and every classroom on the first floor.

Come on, Jacob. Where are you?

I hold on to the handkerchief as if it's magic, but I don't believe in magic. I *do* believe I'll find Jacob though. I have to.

When I get to the third floor, the air feels hotter. The sound of horses trotting along the cobblestones reaches my ears, mixed with the cries from street sellers.

'Buy a box o' matches!'

'Sweet oranges; three a penny, sweet oranges!'

I creep down the hall, peering into each classroom. It gets hotter, until I have to remove my jumper. Horse dung perfumes the air. I *must* be close. The end of the hall flickers like a dodgy TV as I reach the last door.

This has to be it.

I look inside and see row upon row of hospital beds.

Tucked in the furthest corner is Jacob. I rush in.

'Jacob! You're all right!'

'Isaiah, my friend, you're visiting, how miraculous!' The black-and-white colour flickers. *'You found my handkerchief?'*

I reach his bedside. 'I found it. What happened at the workhouse? How did you get away from the fire?'

'Mr Moore was so very angry. It was this protest that was the final straw. I had a plan to cause enough commotion so we'd be moved to the Mayfair workhouse.'

'The one with the Christmas dinners?'

'Exactly. It might not be perfect, but anything is better than Cricklewood. We stuffed the fireplaces to create enough smoke. The smoke never stopped! When Mr Moore discovered us, he tried to lock us away again in the dormitories, but in the struggle a loose cloth caught on fire. It was all an unfortunate accident. It has been our brutal but necessary route to freedom. There are talks of Mr Moore being investigated and Cricklewood being closed for good.'

Maybe the fire was Jacob's escape after all. I hand back the handkerchief. 'I think you should keep this . . . since you'll be seeing your dad very soon. Did you get my note?'

'Yes. Where is he?' Jacob jumps out of his bed, hacking into the handkerchief. 'Where is my father?'

'Are you all right?'

'Perfectly. Just some smoke inhalation, but I'll be making a full recovery.'

'Your dad's in the room right below this one. He's been asking for you.'

'I must go to him before the nurses return me back to my bed.' Jacob flickers some more as he holds out his hand for me to shake. 'It was a great pleasure to make your acquaintance, Isaiah.

This belongs to you.' Jacob puts the handkerchief back inside my palm. *'Goodbye for now, friend.'*

'And this belongs to you,' I say, returning the golden fountain pen to its rightful owner. 'Bye for now to you too, friend.'

Once the classroom goes back to normal, I head downstairs to Mr Paterson's. And through the window – just for an instant – I see Jacob and his father are hugging.

Chapter Forty-Three

Dad is on the sofa with opened letters on the side table by him. The bags under his eyes have darkened.

I put the coffee in front of him and a hot chocolate for myself. Dad throws the blanket over so it covers both of us.

'Do you know how proud I am of you, Isaiah?' he says suddenly.

'Course I do,' I reply, stretching my legs in front of me. 'I'm amazing.'

Dad snorts. 'Not a modest bone in your body. You get that from your mother. Right, I have some good news and some *not* so good news.'

'Good news first.'

'Citizens Advice managed to stop the eviction, so we get to stay here for the time being while they challenge it.'

Then Dad hands me two letters without saying a word. I skim-read both.

Reference number: 234889
Your Personal Independence Payment Decision

Thank you for your claim for Personal Independence Payment. We've considered your claim but have decided you don't qualify for Personal Independence Payment.

If you would like to discuss the decision further, please contact the number below.

I leave that letter and look at the other one. It's a certificate with a court stamp on it.

DIVORCE CERTIFICATE
This certifies that
Matthew Oni & Amma Oni
ended their marriage

I'm holding my parents' divorce certificate.

'I'm going to fight it,' Dad states.

I know he's not talking about the divorce but the assessment decision, but I ask anyway. 'Which one?'

Dad squeezes my shoulder. 'Your mother and I will always love you and try to do the best by you.'

'And the assessment decision?'

'I'm going to appeal it.' Dad's voice is firm. 'They want me to provide all this "evidence" to show why what they wrote in the assessment is a lie. I'm going to give them what they want and then some.'

Dad points to all the other papers on the table: his discharge letter from the hospital, notes from the doctor, physiotherapy letters and stacks of prescriptions and bills.

'Isaiah, there's one thing I want to ask of you,' he says. 'They need a letter from family as part of the evidence. You don't have to do it, but if you want to, that would be much appreciated. The letter is to explain how you help me sometimes and what would happen if you weren't here.'

Every single letter I wrote to Jacob was practice for this one.

'I'll write it, Dad,' I reply. 'And I'll make it the best letter they've ever seen, so they'll *have* to change their minds.'

'That's my boy.'

Chapter Forty-Four

I knock on Mrs Morris's door and wait with Dad. The door opens a few seconds later.

'Thanks for coming in, Mr Oni and Isaiah. I won't keep you out of class for too long,' she says, gesturing to the two seats in front of her desk.

Dad wipes sweat from his forehead. 'Thanks for having us, Mrs Morris.'

'Let's get right to it,' she replies. 'Isaiah, your father and I have spoken, so this meeting is for you. Have you heard of the young carers programme?'

'Uh . . . yeah, I think so. You spoke about it in an assembly one time.'

'You've always had a great memory.' She hides a smile. 'The school believes that because of all you do for your father, you are eligible for support with the young carers programme. The school would like to support both of you. How does that sound, Isaiah?'

I look at Dad and he nods. 'How does that sound, son?'

'It sounds . . . all right?'

It sounds better than all right. 'Can you tell me more about the programme?'

'Yes, I'd be delighted to.' She smiles fully this time and takes out a piece of paper to write on, as well as some official-looking forms. 'To start with, we want to put interventions in place for you: applying for funding, choosing a designated member of staff as your go-to person and creating your own personal schedule, so you don't miss any more school . . .'

'Isaiah, grab your seat,' Mr Paterson says. 'We're just finishing up on our Victorian exhibition debrief and . . . celebrating our dream team!'

The class claps for Kesia and me as I sit down. When everyone is working, Mr Paterson pulls me to one side. 'Has Mrs Morris spoken to you about the programme?'

'Yes, sir. I chose you as my designated staff member.'

Mr Paterson shrinks away in fake horror. 'Noooo.'

'You're not funny, sir.' But I laugh because that *was* funny.

'Have you been speaking to my mum? I'm hilarious.' Mr Paterson's lowers his voice, so only I can hear him. 'Please come to me if you ever need to talk or have questions. I mean it.'

'Thanks, sir. I will.'

'Do the wonderful dream team know which private viewing at the museum they'll be treating their friends and family to?'

Kesia looks at me before answering for both of us. 'Yeah, we're going for the Black inventors and innovators exhibition.'

Epilogue

One month later

'Isaiah, look at this one,' Fredrick says, pointing to one of the inventors. 'I didn't know a Black person invented peanut butter. I love peanut butter!'

'George Washington Carver invented over three hundred uses for peanuts but not actual peanut butter.'

'Yeah, yeah. As long as I can have it on my toast.'

Uncle Kwame grips my shoulders, smiling across at my dad. 'And Isaiah will be in an exhibition like this one day. Mark my words.'

Dad smiles. 'You already know it.'

Mum calls me; I slip outside to take the call. 'Hey, Mum.'

'Hi, Isaiah. Where are you?'

'I'm at the exhibition.'

'Oh yes, that was today. How are you enjoying it? Who did you end up inviting?'

'It's great. Uncle Kwame, Kieran, Kieran's mum, Fredrick and Clarice. She's—'

'*The woman your father's seeing, I know, he's told me. I'm glad to hear that you're being looked after. I can't wait to see you in person in a few months.*'

'Me too!'

Mum bought a ticket for me to spend a few weeks with her in Berlin. I can't wait.

'Are you sure you're OK with me staying with Dad?' I ask. There's a long pause before she answers.

'*You've built something special there in Shepten – anyone can see it. I can't take you away from that, but that doesn't mean I don't miss you.*'

'I miss you too, Mum.'

'*We'll have plenty of time during the summer to spend quality time together. I can't wait. I'll let you get back to the exhibition. Speak soon. Love you.*'

'Bye, Mum.'

I wander off to look at another exhibit, bumping into Kesia on the way. 'Are you stalking me?'

She bumps again on purpose this time. 'No, you're stalking *me*,' she says, then laughs. 'Isaiah, what are you looking at?'

'That's why I couldn't find his death date before!'

Jacob changed his name.

I smile widely as I stand in front of a Black innovator that I know personally. One who has changed my life, even though we were born nearly two hundred years apart. He doesn't go by Jacob Ephraim Akintola any more but by a different name.

Jacob Isaiah-Akintola.

'Look who it is,' I say as Kesia's eyes light up with amazement and then pride. 'He's actually used my name.'

Jacob Isaiah-Akintola was an innovator and social reformer. He was crucial in influencing government policies on the reduction of poverty that led to a range of social reforms in the late 1800s.

'He did it. He made a difference like he always wanted to do,' I say.

'Do you know how cool this is? We *knew* him . . . like actually *knew* him.'

I smirk. 'Well, it's me who actually knew him. You were more like an assistant.'

'Whatever, Isaiah.' She pats my hand like I am a small child. 'If that's what you think.'

Uncle Kwame calls over to Kesia, signalling that we should go outside. *What's going on?* 'Ermm, I bet you can't beat me outside,' she says.

'You're on!' I run through the building, leaving her behind, but I stop once I see my friends and other people I know waiting outside. Uncle Kwame, Kieran, Kieran's mum, Darius, Fredrick, Kesia, Mr Lim, Clarice, and all the other people I fixed things for in the building. They're all standing there, waiting for me.

Dad comes to stand beside me with a matching confused face. 'What's all of this?'

'Isaiah, do you remember when Darius set up a GoFundMe to help make his EP?' Kieran asks.

'Yeah, I remember that.'

'We all set up one. This time for you and your dad,' Darius explains. 'It's for rent payments and anything else you need.'

Dad shifts uncomfortably beside me. 'What are you saying? We . . . we didn't ask for any of this. Are our pictures online?'

'Wait, brother.' Uncle Kwame steps forward. 'We would *never* do anything like that.'

'We made it anonymous,' Kesia adds.

'I drew a picture of you and your dad.' Kieran points to himself. 'And Darius made an animated video and recorded the music for it.'

I face Mr Lim, Clarice and the other people from our block. 'How did you all find out?'

Darius puts up his hand sheepishly. 'It's why I suggested you fixed furniture in the block. These people know you. They care about you.'

'We've raised two thousand pounds so far,' Fredrick says, showing us the GoFundMe account on his phone.

'And it keeps growing too,' Kesia adds.

'I don't know what to say,' Dad starts, and looks at me.

'Someone once told me that I should live each day like it's my last and appreciate the good people . . . however uncivilised. So . . . thanks,' I say.

Dad laughs long and hard at that. It's a laugh I've not heard in a really long time. 'Yes, what Isaiah said.'

Acknowledgements

I want to thank God first, as always, for helping me get through this writing process.

Thank you to Lauren Gardner for being with me right from the beginning of this journey.

To Rumbi, thanks so much again for an amazing cover! I want to thank my team at Hachette: Polly Lyall Grant, Lizzie Clifford, Samuel Perrett, Laura Pritchard, Emily Thomas and Bec Gillies.

Next, I want to acknowledge Ingrid, Jeanna and Lia, who shared with me their courageous stories, thank you.

To Hux, you were one of the first people I spoke to about living with a disability. Thank you so much for your insights, sharing your story and pointing me in the right direction.

To all the wonderful historians who read my work and answered my many questions. Thank you to Dr Julian North, Dr Samantha Shave, Dr Ryan Hanley, Dr Katie Donington and Dr Nicholas Radburn.

To my wonderful sensitivity readers Hayley, Demi and Tonya, thank you. Also, thank you to Omose Agboaye for sharing more on your experience with sickle cell.

And finally, a huge thank you to my friends and family, as always, for your support and help!

Rachel Faturoti is a writer, editor and poet with a passion for broadening the scope of authentic Black representation in YA and children's fiction. She believes it's important for readers to see themselves portrayed well in stories. Rachel's favourite books are *Skellig*, *Coraline* and *A Monster Calls*.

Also available
as an audiobook

Have you read . . .?